Magpie

Also available from Eve Ainsworth:

Lost

For older readers:

7 Days
Crush
Damage
Tender

Magpie

Eve Ainsworth

■SCHOLASTIC

Published in the UK by Scholastic Children's Books, 2021
Euston House, 24 Eversholt Street, London, NW1 1DB, UK
A division of Scholastic Limited.

London – New York – Toronto – Sydney – Auckland
Mexico City – New Delhi – Hong Kong

SCHOLASTIC and associated logos are trademarks and/or
registered trademarks of Scholastic Inc.

ISBN 978 1407 18545 3

A CIP catalogue record for this book
is available from the British Library.

Printed by CPI Group (UK) Ltd, Croydon, CR0 4YY
Papers used by Scholastic Children's Books are made
from wood grown in sustainable forests.

1 3 5 7 9 10 8 6 4 2

This is a work of fiction. Names, characters, places, incidents
and dialogues are products of the author's imagination or are used
fictitiously. Any resemblance to actual people, living or dead,
events or locales is entirely coincidental.

www.scholastic.co.uk

Ella.
Words cannot do you justice. You are amazing
in every way. Never forget that.
Love you always

xxx

Chapter One

Smells always make me remember.

Whenever I smell freshly cut grass, wet mud or that freshness in the air after rain, I'm taken back to the house we shared with Ross – the big one just outside London, with the long, thin garden and tiny allotment at the end. I loved that old house so much. It was tall and grand, like something from a TV programme. I thought we were lucky to be living in a place with white-painted bricks and a bright red door. Even the hallway was grand, with its black-and-white diamond floor tiles and sweeping staircase.

It was a house I thought we would live in for ever. Ross told us it was our home and I believed him.

I believed too many things. . .

But those same smells remind me of what happened there. My stomach clenches and suddenly the nice memories are washed away and I struggle to bring them back. Instead I see Ross's face again – his eyes angry, his mouth moving as he hisses out those horrible, unkind words.

I don't want to remember those things.

Other smells.

When I smell stale tobacco or fried food, I think of the last place we lived, without Ross. By then it was just us – me, Mum, Henry and Alice. All of us squashed together in one room of a shared house, as the smells drifted in from other families. It wasn't bad exactly, but the competing smells reminded us that this home was never really *ours*. Our space belonged to many others, all waiting for something better. If desperation was a smell, then it was the smell of that cramped, stuffy house. It was hard not to choke on it.

And now we are here, in our new house. Something that's ours.

It should be perfect. It's all we ever wanted. We have dreamed of this. Except it's not. It smells funny to me. Mum doesn't believe me when I say that, but it does. The previous tenants lived here for over forty years. The carpets are thin and floral, and the paint choices are . . . questionable. But none of that matters. It's ours and that's the main thing.

Mum says with a bit of scrubbing and some fresh paint, this will be the home that we always wanted.

It's the *smell* that's the problem. Deep and musky, it's so hard to describe, but it kind of gets down the back of my throat and makes me want to cough. I hate it so much; give me the scent of the sea any day.

I asked her if the last owners died here and she gave me a tired look. It was a genuine question! Henry was fascinated though. He thinks that there might be ghosts. Apparently ghosts are really cool.

But I can't ignore the smell. It smells wrong.

I try to convince myself that a smell means nothing. Just because it makes my stomach tense again, just because my skin prickles – it doesn't mean that anything is going to happen. We've been told time and time again that we are safe now. Ross can't hurt us any more. I have to believe everything is OK now.

So why is that so hard?

It's the weekend. I'm lying on my new bed in my new room. At the moment it's all mine, until Amy is a little bigger, when she will be sharing with me.

It's an L-shape, so we've put my bed under the window. I can sit there and look out at the street outside. Not that there's much to see: a bit of communal grass where Henry likes to kick his ball and a tiny, square car park.

I haven't seen many other kids around here yet. On one side there is an old man with a hearing aid who whistles. Sometimes he waves at us from his back garden.

The house on the other side of us is neat and tidy with pretty flowers in the front garden. I've seen the woman that lives there a few times. She's kind of middle-aged-looking with bright grey hair and slanted eyes that remind me of a cat and every time she sees me, she wrinkles her nose and turns away.

Perhaps I stink like this house. Maybe I'm absorbing it like some kind of sponge. That'll impress the girls at school. Here comes weirdo Alice again, only this time she's wearing her new scent – "rotten veg". At least it would give them something else to fixate on for a change. Even though I've been at the school since we moved back to town, I'm still treated like the new girl. I guess some things are hard to change.

My room is pretty empty. We've never had much stuff, partly because of all the moving around we've done. When we left Ross that last time, we snuck out in the night with just a few clothes and what Mum said were "the essentials". There were so many things that we left behind – books, photos, drawings – all gone. Now I'm just surrounded by space and blank walls. Mum says in time we'll fill it all up again. That it might take time, but in the end our lives will start to feel normal.

I hope she's right.

My phone vibrates on the bed beside me. A message from Alfie. I swipe it open.

Hey! Game cancelled tomorrow so that means I can FINALLY come and see your new house! Are you around?

I smile. It's probably fair to say Alfie is my best mate, but he's obsessed with football, so the only time I see him is when a game is cancelled. Why can't I have a mate who's into reading or gaming or something? At least he'd be around more. It's been two months in this new house and he's not been over yet. Still, I can't blame him. We're right the other side of town. And there's not much here – just rows of identical-looking houses and some scraps of green. There is a cool play park that Henry likes though, which is better than we had before. I look around the room, with its dodgy paintwork and bare walls. I can't decide whether I want him here or not. Alfie has a big house with nice things in it. My fingers hesitate over the keys. *Do I want him here?*

But like a drifting cloud, the thought passes. Of course I want him here. This is *Alfie*. My best and most annoying friend. He totally gets it.

What's more – I've missed him.

Cool! I type back. *Come over after lunch.*

Then I send him my address.

Number 12, Ryelands.

The address of my actual house. It doesn't matter what it looks like, I think. It's a home.

It's mine.

I glance out of the window and smile. This small piece of land and everything around it is our life now. We have green! An outdoors of our own. I have to feel grateful. Things could have been very different.

It's only as I turn away that I see that figure standing by our garden gate. I lean forward, tweaking the curtain a little. The figure turns away from the house, so I can't see their face at all.

Then they walk on. It's just a passer-by, I

think. Someone who realized they have the wrong house.

But I stay rooted on the spot for a few minutes more, watching, just to be sure.

I like to be on the move. I don't even like being indoors for too long. I think I've always felt this way, but it got worse when we lived with Ross. All I could think about was getting outside and away from him. It's like a buzzing inside my legs. I feel like I always need to get up and go out in the fresh air or else I'll go mad. I don't even care if it's raining.

It drives Mum mad. She calls me a "free spirit". She says that I should have been born a cat, or a wolf, free to roam the land with no one else bothering me.

Alfie, my friend, always says I'm more like a bird.

"Birds are strong, but they're fragile too," he said to me once when we were hanging out, grinning in that easy way of his. "Like you."

I scowled at him. "I'm not fragile. . ."

Alfie just shrugged, still smiling in that annoying way. "If you say so."

"I'm not a bird," I told him. "Birds are weak and vulnerable. They soon get eaten up."

"Not if they're quick. . ." Alfie said. "And you're quick." I didn't say anything else after that. I didn't want to admit it to him, but part of me quite liked being compared to a bird. I'd love to be able to fly. I'd be truly free. I could go wherever I wanted. I'd never feel trapped again.

Also, I knew how much Alfie loved birds. Maybe he was complimenting me, in his weird way.

At least, I like to think he was.

Downstairs, Mum is cooking dinner. She's humming happily as she chops an onion and throws it into a pan along with some vegetables. The smell that soon fills the room is warm and comforting.

Out of our entire new house, she loves our kitchen the most. I swear she actually started crying when she first saw the oven. I understand,

I guess. In the shared house we just had a microwave and the kitchen was always packed, so we would eat our meals sitting on our beds, balancing plates on our laps.

Mum looks up as I walk in and smiles. She looks tired and her eyes are red, but I think that's Amy's doing – she was up in the night again teething. "This won't be long," she says, gesturing at the saucepan. "I'm making a spag bol. Your favourite."

"Nice," I say, trying to sound cheerful. I keep thinking of that figure by our front gate. I wish I'd seen their face, just to be sure.

I drop into the chair opposite Amy. She's in a high chair, stacking bricks with one hand and sucking on a biscuit with the other. "Where's Henry?" I ask.

"Out in the garden," Mum says, grinning and pushing her long hair back behind her ears. "Exploring apparently."

"Cool." I nick a bit of chopped pepper from the chopping board and pop it into my mouth. "Alfie is coming over tomorrow."

Mum turns to me. I swear her whole face lights up. "Is he? Great! I've not seen him for ages."

Alfie and my mum get on really well. Mum always says Alfie reminds her a bit of someone she knew a long time ago. They were best friends too apparently. Mum used to live in this town when she was teenager. It must be strange for her to come back. This was the town where she finished her education, where she met my dad and where she finally moved away to London when that didn't work out. Mum doesn't like talking about her childhood much. I know she grew up in care homes and I know that she was happiest in this place. Whenever I ask anything else, she just gets cross with me and tells me not to talk about it.

"He's had football tournaments and stuff," I say.

My fingers trace across the rough wood of our kitchen table. Alfie's dad gave it to us. I love the feel of it against my skin. "He has another trial coming up."

"Really?" Mum says, turning back and stirring the sauce. "He's so good, isn't he? Which team is it for?" I snort. Like Mum would know *any* football team. She calls it the "dullest game on earth" (not that she'd tell Alfie that).

"Hey, I like football," Mum says. "Go on, who are they?"

"I can't remember," I say. "But they're good. Premiership, I think. . ."

Mum laughs softly. "You're no more interested in football than I am."

I frown, my fingers digging into the wood a little harder. It's not that I don't like football. Actually, it can be quite fun watching Alfie play. But sometimes it feels like it's all Alfie cares about these days. He's too busy to hang out.

I give myself a little shake. I'm being selfish. I was so lucky to meet Alfie when we moved here. He was the only one who seemed to understand me, who bothered to get to know me. It's not like he's had an easy ride of it either. After his mum died he struggled to cope; he even stopped playing football and he's only just got back into it again. I shouldn't be jealous that he has something he cares about. I know how good it is for him.

The back door crashes open and into my thoughts, and Henry runs in. He looks a complete state. There are streaks of mud across his red cheeks and he has a couple of twigs sticking out of his hair, like tiny bent-up horns. He always looks like such a mucky little thing with his sticky-up hair and bright red cheeks, but it only makes me love him even more.

"Alice!" he cries when he sees me, his eyes bright. "I've made such a cool den. Come and see."

I let him lead me back into the garden, picking our way over the broken paving and ducking under the sagging washing line. Despite it being a mess still, full of bags of rubbish and piles of leaves, we love it out here. We had a garden before, but that was Ross's and he kept it immaculate. In Ross's garden the walls felt too high and everything was too "pretty" so we could never properly relax or run wild. So for Henry especially, this garden is the most exciting thing ever.

It's his new playground.

Right by the fence there is a small, spindly tree and Henry has hooked one of his huge old blankets over the lower branches to make a makeshift tent.

"Look," he says, pointing. "It's a camp. We can sleep out here at night."

"It could get chilly," I say. "Muddy, too."

"So? It's an adventure!" His eyes sparkle. "I could stay out all night and look at the stars."

Henry loves the stars, or anything to do with space. It's his latest obsession. He says when he's older he wants to fly to the moon. Or Uranus (which makes him giggle every time he says it because it sounds rude). I guess he's a bit like me in that way, he thrives on being outside.

"I want Alfie to see my camp," Henry says. "He'll like it. He went camping, didn't he?"

"He did. A few weeks ago."

He went with his dad. Their first holiday since his mum had died. I had told him that he would love it, that it would do him good. And I was right – he *had* loved it. He had come back buzzing, talking about all the fishing they had done together and the long chats they'd had late at night.

Mum isn't the only member of my family who adores Alfie. I look at Henry's hopeful little face.

"Is that why you've made this?" I say gently. "So you can be like Alfie?"

"Noooo. . ." Henry's protest is too loud.

I grin. "Well, he's coming to visit tomorrow. So you can show him your tent then and see what he thinks."

Henry beams. Then he nestles himself inside his den. I squeeze in beside him, pulling the blanket over us. I take in a big gulp of clear, crisp air and I love the feeling of my lungs being full of fresh goodness.

"I like it here. It's really nice," he whispers.

"What, in your tent?"

"No. . ." He shakes his head and the tree moves slightly with him. "I like it here, in our new house."

"I do too," I reply softly.

Except for the smell inside. I shiver.

"We're safe here, aren't we, Alice?" he says. His

voice is so quiet, I can barely hear him. "No one bad can find us here."

"We're safe, Henry. We're totally safe."

And, right there under the trees, I almost believe it.

Chapter Two

The thing about Ross is that he wasn't always bad. It's important for me to remember that.

I used to really like him. It wasn't just Mum who believed in him, it was all of us, and if I'm honest, sometimes I think I was the biggest fool of all.

Mum always said that he "swept her off her feet" when she first met him. He was charming and funny and polite and clever. Ross was there to save us. Me and Mum. He was going to give us a better life long before Henry and Amy came along. He was going to give us the life "we deserved".

I can't pinpoint the time when things changed. When I started to see the other side. Things changed gradually, so gradually in fact that it became easier to accept the new normal than question it.

In the early days I remember Mum spoke up more. She was far more confident and not scared to snap at Ross if he was in a bad mood, or tell him to chill out. I knew Ross didn't like it. I could tell from the hard expression in his face and his short, icy replies. Back then, I used to beg Mum to be nice to him, not to make him angry. I didn't want her to cause trouble, to destroy our new-found "happiness". I heard his rages later, while I was curled up in bed, I heard him telling her not to "upset him" or "disrespect him". He would remind her then of all the things he had done for us – all the sacrifices he had made. Mum soon learnt it was much easier not to speak up. It was better to stay silent. After all, why rock the boat?

In the early days, I could almost pretend that we were a normal family like every other kid had at school. And Ross liked me. That mattered! He was always pleased with me whenever I "stuck up for him". He'd buy me nice things and call me his "princess", he'd ruffle my hair and give me his warmest grin. He looked so handsome then, with his designer clothes and his sharp, short haircuts. He almost looked like a model from an advert – all smooth and twinkly eyed. I liked the way he would smile at me like he was so proud of me. I liked the way his eyes creased and his face flooded with warmth. It made me feel special.

"You're a good girl, Alice," he'd say. "You understand how things are."

Except I didn't. Not really. I didn't understand why Ross could be lovely one minute and so angry the next.

And I could never be his "good girl" – because, in the end, I was the reason Mum left him for good.

That night, I'm brushing my teeth before bed when I see them again. The person I saw earlier. This time they have moved to the other end of the road, and they're leaning up against a tree. It's dark outside so it's really tricky to make them out properly. I think they are taller than me. Skinny too. The hood they are wearing is up and I can't see their face, but I swear they are looking straight at me.

I step back quickly. My heart is hammering in my chest.

Mum told us we were safe. So did the police. But what if they were wrong? I know Ross, know how persistent he can be. Ross could get anything if he wanted to – including our new address. I lean forward again. I have to see if it's him. But the figure has gone. I check both left and right, but there's no sign at all.

It's like they were never there at all.

I shake my head. *Stupid.* I'm being so stupid.

So why do I still feel so sick and shaky inside?

The doorbell goes, bang on one the next day. Henry shrieks loudly.

"He's here!"

Henry runs to the door and tugs it open, beaming. "Alfie!" he squeals. "Yay!"

"Henry, my little man," I hear Alfie say. "How are things with you?"

I join him in the hall, putting my hands on his shoulders and gently easing him to one side so that Alfie can get past.

"C'mon, mate, aren't you going to let Alfie in?" I say softly.

"Have you brought your football?" Henry asks, jumping from foot to foot in excitement.

"I haven't got my ball, Henry. I need a break. My legs are killing me from training yesterday," Alfie says. "Besides, I came to see your house, not have a kick around."

"About time too," I reply, grinning at him.

Alfie is a good head taller than me and lean. He looks like someone who is naturally good at sport – you can just tell by their whole attitude and the way they hold themselves. Even standing here in front of us, I notice he is flexing his leg slightly – like he's ready to go for a run, or boot a ball across the road. The opposite of me. All I can do is run fast. A really nice thing about Alfie is that even though he's talented, with scouts coming to watch his games and talk of scholarships, he doesn't act all cocky. He's friends with the popular, sporty kids but he's nice to everyone at school. His other best mate is Ben after all. Ben isn't sporty at all. He's arty and a bit "out there" but is also dead funny. I love it when Ben spends time with us too. He makes everything much more fun and interesting.

"Come inside and look around," Henry says, pulling at Alfie's arm. "I have my own bedroom. It's really big."

We take Alfie on a tour of the house. It's hard not to be excited. This is all ours! We are finally normal like everyone else. I just hope he doesn't notice the smell. I gave it a good spritz with air freshener before he arrived. I walk him around the small living room, proudly showing off the space that is all ours. Then I lead him upstairs. Henry is keen to show him his bedroom. Alfie laughs out loud when he sees the assorted football posters stuck up on the wall all haphazard.

"I want a football duvet, but Mum says I can't," Henry moans.

"She didn't say that exactly." I turn to Alfie to explain. "It's just the money – you know."

Alfie nods. Of course he knows. He always does.

"Listen, mate, I might have an old one at home. Shall I have a look?"

Henry shrieks with joy. "Yes, please!"

I feel a bit weird when he finally looks in my room – it doesn't look like a girl's bedroom, really, with its bare walls and battered old furniture. But he just grins and says, "Nice. This is so cool."

"You think?"

"Yeah! Of course. It's all yours!"

We end up back where we started, in the living room.

Alfie looks around again, a wide smile plastered on his face. "You have so much space."

"That's because we have no furniture," I say.

It's true. Mum managed to find us a sofa, table and some chairs at the charity shop, and of course Alfie's dad helped out with the dining room table and chairs and a few other bits, but there is still so much space to fill. Currently our tiny TV is sitting on an upturned cardboard box.

"It's nice though..." Alfie says, nodding slowly. "Like, sometimes a place can get too full of stuff. Do you know what I mean? It can feel overcrowded and small. This feels kind of fresh."

"Really? It doesn't smell it," I say without meaning to.

Alfie looks at me. "What do you mean?"

"Alice thinks it's smelly in here. But I don't and neither does Mummy," Henry tells him, glaring at me. "I think it's really nice. I love it here."

"So do I," I reply quickly. "But – but there is a weird smell. Can't you tell?"

Alfie frowned. "No – not really. It's just an old house smell. It smells a bit like my grandad's." He smiles at me. "You're just not used to it. You've spent too much time outside."

I shrug. "Maybe."

We walk into the kitchen. Alfie grins when he sees his old table. He pulls out a chair and sits down, and I do the same.

"I'm glad Dad gave this to you guys – it was sad seeing it in our garage. I used to sit here all the time when I was a kid." His hand skims the wood and I see something pass across his face. "Mum used to sit there and do her crosswords. I swear you can still see her pen marks on it."

"I'm sorry," I say. I know how much Alfie misses his mum, even though he doesn't like to talk about it too much. Sometimes I struggle to find the right things to say. How can I? No one I've loved has ever died – well, except my cat and I guess that's not quite the same.

Sometimes I feel like Ross has died. The "nice" Ross. The one that me and Mum fell in love with. Henry and Amy's dad too, of course. Henry doesn't even talk about him any more. I don't think he can stand to.

"It's OK. I'm just glad it's getting used," Alfie says. "To be honest I always liked this table more than the new one Dad got. He loves changing things around. I think it helps him. . ." He pauses and looks around the kitchen. "This is a big room too, bigger than ours. I bet your mum loves it in here."

I smile. "Yes – she's so excited. She said she'll start baking again and everything."

Mum used to love making cakes and biscuits before. She hasn't been able to for so long.

"Where is she now?" he asks.

"She's taken Amy to the park, but she won't be long. She really wants to see you."

"Wait, I want you to see my room again," Henry says, running over and taking Alfie's hand. "I have a new football book. Let me show you!"

"OK. OK." Alfie laughs, letting Henry drag him away.

I laugh as they leave. I look out at the garden. From here I can glimpse a couple of birds hopping on the small bent-up tree. Above me I can hear the thump, thump, thump of Henry's footsteps and his loud giggles. I smile. Then, quick as a blink, the figure from last night flickers into my mind. I shut it out again but it's there, like a shadow against the sun. I lay my hands flat on the table and sigh. Will it ever be possible for me to feel truly happy? Or will I be worrying for the rest of my life?

*

A little later, we sit on the low wall in the garden, with the warmer afternoon sun beating down on us. "We should go in soon," Alfie says, wiping his forehead. "I don't want to fry out here."

"Yeah – in a bit." I tip my face up to the sky, loving the warmth on my skin. "But it's nice out here, isn't it? Really quiet. You can just sit and think."

"I guess. But then you would sit outside all day if you could."

I smile. "At least it smells better than indoors."

"I really don't get the problem, I think the house smells just fine," Alfie says.

"Yeah – you need your nose testing."

A brief silence takes over. I don't mind. It's nice just to sit and be at peace for a bit. Sometimes everything seems so mad and rushy, you can forget just to be still and breathe.

After a while, I glance at him. "I guess you've been busy lately?"

"The football has taken over a bit," he says matter-of-factly. "Training is three times a week now and I have to fit in schoolwork too."

"You're doing so well though."

He shrugs. "You are," I tell him firmly. "When you think how you were a few months back."

When I first met Alfie, he was a ghost. An unhappy, shrunken ghost who didn't want to be near anyone. But now I can see he's coming alive again. Slowly, slowly he's getting better.

"Yeah. It's all good. You and Ben have really helped." He pauses. "Well, Ben has tried, but I think he's a bit distracted at the moment."

"What's on his mind at the moment? Is he still fixated on his artwork?"

Alfie shrugs. "I think so. I reckon he likes some girl too. I'm going to try and found out. He's been acting more weird then ever recently."

I smile. Ben is so different from Alfie in that he's pretty loud and funny and wears his heart on his sleeve – whereas Alfie is more calm and chilled. Alfie always rolls his eyes when he talks about Ben, like he can't believe the latest mad thing he's done, but I know for a fact he wouldn't be without him.

"You're doing well too," he says, turning to

look at me. "This place. Settling down after that shared house. . ."

"Yeah, finally."

"And you're safe," he says. "He can't find you here."

There's a silence and then I say, softly, "What if he can?"

Alfie sits up straight. "The police have an injunction, right? That means he has to leave you and your family alone."

"But what if. . ." I swallow. "What if he doesn't listen?"

"He will. It's the law."

"But what if. . ." I pause. I want to tell him about the person outside the house. But then I realize how stupid and paranoid it makes me sound.

"What if what?" he asks.

"Nothing," I say, shaking my head.

"You would tell me, wouldn't you? If you were worried about something? Because I'll always try and help," Alfie says softly.

I look back at him. "Would you? Really?"

"Of course. You're my mate, aren't you?"
I grin. "And you're my mate too."
And it is one thing I am truly grateful for.

Chapter Three

I can still remember meeting Ross for the first time. I was only about five when Mum introduced him to me.

I wasn't sure about him at first but only because I was really shy. It had always just been me and my mum before. I hadn't known my own dad at all – he'd left before I was born. Mum would always say, "It's me and you now, kid" – that we were lone warriors – and I liked that idea a lot. It made me feel like we were important and didn't need anyone else at all.

So when Ross came along with his dark hair,

smart suits and shiny car, I wasn't happy about it at all, apparently. I think I wanted him to leave us alone. We were doing perfectly OK on our own, thank you very much; we didn't need anyone else.

But Mum told me later that we weren't OK, not really. I didn't realize because I was too little. I do remember my shoes were always too tight and Mum was often struggling to top up the electric meter card, so some nights we had to go to bed early to keep warm. I liked those nights though, me and Mum huddled up together under her thin duvet, whispering stories to each other and trying not to listen to the creaks from the ancient water pipes.

When Ross came along, all those problems suddenly disappeared. He bought me brand new shoes and trainers straight away – proper Nike ones instead of the tatty cheap ones Mum got me from the charity shop.

I don't remember much about those times, but what I can remember is good. I know Ross took us out for dinner lots. We'd go for pub lunches and he'd tell us to order whatever we wanted. He would tease Mum for checking the prices and worrying. He would laugh at how fast I ate. It was because I was scared it would be taken away from me, but I didn't tell him that. Mum waited a while before we moved in with him; she said she "wanted to be sure". When we finally did, I was so excited, but scared too. This was a big deal. We were moving to London, miles away from home. Ross had a huge house. He let me pick my own bedroom. I couldn't believe it – me and Mum had always shared before. How could my life change so quickly? Ross and Mum even said I could pick my own bed, curtains, a new rug. . . They wanted my space to be all mine.

"All mine?" I said, bouncing on the bed happily. Already I was imagining how wonderful it would look.

Mum stroked my hair and smiled at me.

"Things are going to be so different now," she said.

Ross took my hand then, and looked me straight in the eye.

He said, "I might not be your real dad, but I'm

going to try really hard to be a good dad to you all the same."

Everything inside of me tingled, because I believed him. Or at least I really, really wanted to believe him.

I wanted Ross to be my dad.

It was my dream and he knew it. I wanted a dad like everyone else.

But he ended up being our nightmare.

Everyone is in the kitchen when I leave for school on Monday. As usual, Henry is on his second bowl of Weetabix chatting about his day ahead at school and Amy is in a high chair banging bricks together. "Bye, Mum," I say loudly, over the noise.

Mum is sitting at the table looking at her phone, a tiny frown etched on her face. She doesn't bother to look up. "Oh – OK... Have you had breakfast?"

"No time. Have you got my lunch money?"

She nods, still staring at her phone in a worried sort of way, and pushes her wallet towards me.

There's a handful of five- and ten-pence pieces inside. "Mum, is this all you have?" I ask.

"I think so," she says vaguely. "Is it enough?"

I pause. I want to say that it's not enough. I want to say that going into the canteen with a handful of coins will be social death. But it'll only stress her out even more and she's obviously distracted by something else today.

So instead I take a handful of coins and put them in my pocket. It'll be enough to buy some fruit. Or maybe a bread roll.

I walk on my own today. Alfie usually goes in earlier now for practice and I'm never ready in time. When he does go in later he tends to have a gang of other lads in his year with him, and although I like some of them, Ben especially, the others tend to look at me like I'm some kind of annoying little sister. I don't want to feel like I'm a burden to Alfie, someone he has to put up with just because he's nice.

The one thing I liked about the shared house, the last place we lived before here, was that I could walk to school along the beach. Now my journey is all housing estates and long, dull stretches of road. There's not really much to look at around here. It's almost as if this is the part of town that has been neglected and cast aside. You can just tell by the beaten-up roads and the litter scattered across the street. Across the way there is the scarred shell of a burnt-out car. I wonder how it got there. Did it actually crash or did some kids set it alight for a laugh?

Sometimes when we walk past a gang of teenagers, laughing and messing about, Mum gives me a quick, worried look, like she's scared I'm going to suddenly turn into one of them. These are the kids who hardly go to school at all. That hang around the estate smoking, shouting at anyone who passes by. That's Mum's biggest worry – me going off the rails. That's why she likes me being mates with Alfie. He's every mother's dream. I carry on up the main road that runs into the main part of town. As you follow the road, you can see that you are moving away from the estate. The houses are more spaced apart and much grander and bigger. This main road leads all the way through the small town, past our school and then on to the beach. The bus flies past me. One day I might ask Mum for money to take it. When we've sorted ourselves out a bit.

"Alice! Wait up!"

I turn and see that Ben is standing at the end of the road. He lives on this side of town, near to Alfie. I'm not particularly surprised to see him. Ben hates going to school early, unless he has to, so he wouldn't have wanted to walk in with Alfie.

"Hey!" I smile as he walks over to me.

"How's the new house? Alfie says you're settling in OK."

"Yeah. It's not so bad." I wrinkle my nose. "I still think it smells kind of weird, but no one else seems to notice."

"Maybe there's something wrong with your nose then?"

I laugh. "Yeah, maybe."

We are walking comfortably together. I can't help sneaking a sly look at Ben as he strides along beside me. He's taller than Alfie and skinnier, with a mess of dark hair that he usually cuts or colours in wonderful or weird ways. At the moment it's pretty tame and just has a hint of green at the tips. Ben must notice I'm looking and catches my eye. It's then when I notice his eyebrow.

"Oh my god! What have you done?"

He grins back at me. "I was trying to put a line through it, but my arm slipped, so I ended up taking half of it off. It wasn't really the look I was going for. . ."

I cover my mouth, trying not to laugh out loud. "Ben – it looks weird."

He shrugs. "Well, it fits in with my overall vibe then, doesn't it?"

"Don't you care?" I ask. "People will say things..."

He frowns a little. "Not really. I've only ever cared what people I like think about me. The rest can just do one." He pauses. "You don't think I'm weird, do you?"

I can feel my cheeks burning a little. "No – well, a bit. But in a good way."

"Well that's OK then."

It takes about twenty minutes altogether before

we reach the school gates – but that's walking at a much slower pace than usual. Ben never seems to be in a rush. He touches my arm as we arrive.

"I've got to go straight in. I'll catch you later, maybe?"

I smile back. "Yeah, see you later."

My eyes scan the playground. I see the other students milling around, laughing and talking loudly. They are all identical, wearing uniforms, the girls with their black skirts hitched up. I look down at my own uniform. At my skirt with the tatty hem that Mum hasn't had time to fix, at my scuffed school shoes with the too-thick soles that look dead old-fashioned but were half price in the shop. Even my coat doesn't fit. It's bright red and oversized, an old one of Mum's that she told me helpfully "would be perfect for school".

But it's not perfect. None of it is. And neither am I.

I can't be like Ben. It matters to me what others think. I wish it didn't, but it does.

My hands reach up to my hair, wild as ever, and drag it back from my face. I take a deep breath and then, biting the inside of my cheek, I walk in through the gate.

They are waiting outside the form room, gossiping as usual. Esme Reeves and Chloe Dean. I have the misfortune of sharing most of my lessons with them.

To any outsider they probably look innocent enough. Esme is tiny, with bright blue eyes that seem to see right through you. Chloe is taller, athletic. She gets picked first for every event at sports day. Her skirt is always hitched up and her tie is always fashionably short. Chloe could probably still look good if she was wearing an old bin bag. They smile at me as I approach. I've got used to this smile. It's an "oh my god, look at the state of you" kind of smile. It's the "I'm acting like your friend, but actually I can't stand you" look.

Esme and Chloe act like they are sweetness and light. But they are snakes. And I've never liked snakes. They curl around your ankles and bite you when you're not looking.

"Alice!" Esme flashes her white teeth at me. "Look at you!"

Chloe giggles. "You always look so cute in that coat. I mean, it's so *different* – but it makes you look . . . sweet."

The last word hangs between us. Never before has the word "sweet" been used in such a wrong context. Chloe's cool eyes tell me everything. She doesn't think I look sweet at all. She thinks I look awful.

"And your hair. . ." Esme says softly. "We keep saying how cool you are, not bothering to straighten it or anything." She smiles. "It must be so freeing."

They watch me expectantly. "This is just how I am," I say stiffly.

"Of course." Chloe takes a step closer. "And it's great. But if you ever need any, like, style advice—"

"We might be able to help," Esme finishes. "Just bear that in mind."

I push past them to get into the room.

"No thanks," I say as I pass, not bothering to sound polite.

"Oooooh," Chloe says loudly. "That's not nice. We were just trying to help."

"Yeah, Alice." Esme hisses my name behind me, like ice. "You should be nice to us, you know."

She's right, I think, as I sink into an empty desk. I should be nice to them. But right now, I don't have the energy.

The day is no worse than any other day but I still hate it. I can't explain why, not really. I tried talking to Alfie about it once. Being indoors all day, the smell, the noises, the small constricted classrooms – they make me feel sick. Like I'm in the wrong place.

I want grass beneath my feet, not scratched-up lino. I want to be able to tip my head up and look at the sky, not the grim overbearing ceiling with the bright, flickering fluorescent lighting. I want to breath in huge gulps of cool, beautiful air. I want to smell the sea, not stale recycled air.

I can't stand it here. Every minute I'm in school I feel like I'm shrinking away. I don't feel like me any more.

I'm not Alice. I don't want to become like them. Like every other boring person here.

There's only one classroom where I feel happy here. Just one. And it's my last lesson, so the thought of it keeps me going all day.

The art studio is slightly set away from the school in its own little hut. Windows run along both sides and there's a large door at the end that is often propped open. It smells good in there – of wood, paint and the fresh air that drifts in and ruffles our paper as we work.

Our teacher is Ms Monroe. She is quite young, with long dark hair that she wears in a silky plait. As she moves across the room, her plait swings gently from side to side, but not a piece of it is out of place. Ms Monroe is small and neat with beautifully styled clothes and shoes that are so soft that they make no sound as she walks. I don't know what she thinks of me as I clunk over to my seat and crash my stuff down around me, but I'd like to think that she doesn't judge me. She doesn't seem the type.

She seems to actually listen when you talk to her. She never interrupts. She knows everybody's name.

Today we are sketching. It is still life and my

subject is a battered old shoe that I brought in. It's one of Henry's that he's grown out of. Mum put them in a bag for the charity shop, but I fished them out again. They were the last expensive shoes any of us were bought. I wanted to remember the time when we never had to worry about shoes, money or people breaking promises.

Sitting there, sketching in the quiet room, my eyes completely focused on the battered leather and the breeze from the open window behind me tickling my neck, I finally begin to relax. The picture takes shape in front of me. I draw without really thinking at all. For once my mind is completely empty. It's just me and the shoe and the pencil and the paper and the sounds of other kids drawing.

Perhaps there is somewhere in this school where I belong.

Just a little bit.

Chapter Four

I had a friend once, a really good one. Her name was Poppy Granger and she went to the same primary school as me when I was living with Ross. She made up the best games. We were always giggling and telling each other secrets. We were going to be friends for life, we said.

Then Mum left Ross for the first time.

The details are blotchy when I try to remember. I think I've tried to blank so much out over time. Back then, Ross was becoming like a dad to me. It was still only me then. Henry wasn't yet born. I loved Ross fiercely; I felt like I really mattered to him. So when Mum woke me up early one morning and said we were going away for a bit, I was really upset. I didn't want to leave, but she made me. She said we had no choice.

I hated the poky little bedsit that she took us to. It was another place that smelt all wrong – damp and stale like old shoes that had been forgotten at the back of the cupboard. She didn't tell me why we had left, only that "she couldn't be there any more". It didn't make any sense to me. Ross was part of our family now. I missed him so much.

I think I cried myself to sleep every night.

Then Ross came for us. I think I always hoped he would. Mum let him in but her mouth was set in a hard line and she wouldn't look at him; instead she stared at the floor.

We all sat on the bed together.

"I miss you," Ross said softly. He looked over at me. "I miss both of you so much."

He looked different. His normally thickly styled hair was all messed up and falling into his face. His chin was rough with stubble and his eyes looked red raw, like he had been crying for days, just like me. Something inside of me ached.

"I can't do this without you," he said, taking Mum's hand. "Either of you."

Mum was crying softly. "I miss you too."

He sighed. "Then come back with me. Stop being so silly." He laughed gently, shook his head. "It was just an argument. That's all. . ."

"But you hurt me." Mum's voice was sharp. It made me jump.

Had Ross hurt her? I didn't know. But Ross's eyes were wide and innocent; his mouth fell open as if shocked.

"I didn't really, did I? That was nothing, just a tap. I'd never actually hurt you. You wound me a little, Viv." He sighed. "You know how much I love you, don't you? You can't blame me for getting angry sometimes. It's because I love you."

She nodded.

Ross turned to me. I could see tears glistening in his eyes; I'd never seen him look so upset. "I love you too, Alice. You're my little girl. I can't stand being away from you. It's tearing me apart."

Something shattered inside of me. I flung myself into his arms. Breathed in his beautiful, deep heady scent. It smelt like home. My home.

"I want to go back, Mummy," I said. "Please. I want to go back."

Mum had this strange look on her face. She was watching Ross stroke my hair and her eyes widened a little. Then she slowly wiped away her tears.

"OK. We'll go back," she said.

"I'm sorry. It'll be a new start," Ross said. "For all of us. It'll be different this time."

That was the first time we left Ross. Little did I know we would leave a further three times after that. Each time he said the same thing.

"I'm sorry. It'll be different this time."

Each time he lied.

I hang back a bit after we finish art, not keen to rush home. I do this a lot. Ms Monroe never seems to mind. Sometimes I help her tidy up a bit. She never asks me why I'm not in a rush to leave, which is another reason for me liking her.

It's so much easier to get on when I'm not hit with a load of questions.

This afternoon though, I want to finish my drawing.

"Alice. . ." Ms Monroe says. I hadn't noticed her coming over. "That's really impressive. I can't believe you've managed to add so much detail in so little time."

I flush and push the piece of paper away. "It's rubbish. I just like being here, that's all."

Ms Monroe smiles. "That's nice to know." She picks up my work carefully. "And you *are* good at this. In fact you are so good that I think you should come to my art group."

I stare up at her. I knew there was an art group but I thought it was just for older kids.

"Oh – I dunno. . ."

"It's Wednesday after school, mixed years." She looks at me intently. "Ben Richards comes to it – you know him, don't you?"

I nod. "Yeah, he walks to school with me and my friend sometimes. I didn't know he liked art though."

"Oh yes – he's very good."

I blush a little and wonder why I'm suddenly really keen to see just how good he is.

"It might be nice for you to get to know some of the other kids too," she goes on. "I know what it's like moving to a new school." She grins. "My dad was in the army so we were constantly moving from place to place. It was so hard at times. I guess I never felt properly settled."

I shift on my seat, unsure what to say. Words are trapped on my tongue, looking for an escape, but for some reason I hold them back.

"What I'm trying to say," she goes on, "is that I'm here if you ever want to talk to me."

"OK," I mutter.

"And you'll come to art club? This Wednesday?"

"Maybe," I say, slipping off my stool.

Just maybe.

Halfway home along the main road, I cut across to the park. This way I can stroll beside the tiny stream that meanders through it. If you ignore the discarded rubbish in the bushes and the colour of the water, it can look really pretty. I love everything about the place, like the way the wind whips through the low wispy trees, catching my hair as I walk. It makes a lovely rustling sound that makes the whole place come alive somehow. I love the crisp, wet smell of the stream. And I love it that I can drift along in a daze almost, imagining the beautiful birds and tiny animals that are hiding away in the leaves and bushes. I even saw a heron here once, although no one believed me. It was sitting in the stream for ages just looking at me. I haven't seen it since and I'd really love to.

I follow the muddy path towards the small bridge at the end. I'm staring out at the stream and hoping to see the heron when my phone buzzes, twice.

One text from Mum saying *I got sausages for tea* and another from Alfie.

I'm playing a match Saturday 11ish – Dad can pick you up if you fancy it? I could use a friendly face.

I text back straight away

Sounds good. I'll come and send winning vibes.

I don't really like football, but I do like being outdoors in whatever weather, cheering on my friend. Alfie's dad is lovely too, he always makes me laugh and brings a thermos of hot chocolate and cheers Alfie till his throat is hoarse. Sometimes it makes me ache inside when I realize that's what I'm missing – a dad of my own. I try not to think about that for too long.

I come out of the tiny wooded area and back out into the estate. It takes about ten minutes of cutting through the identical-looking streets before I hit my own. My head feels clearer and my feet are lighter. Just seeing a bit of greenery has done that.

I turn up the street that leads to my house. *Mine.* The unsettled feeling still claws at me.

I remember I asked Mum, after we left Ross for the last time, if we'd always be poor now. We were stuck in that awful shared house and had already gone a few months with rubbish meals and little heating. I asked her if it would always be this way. How could we change our circumstances without Ross's help?

We had been walking along the road at the time, on the way to take the kids to the park. She laughed and then said, "It's hard to explain. But when you're in a lower position to start with, it's not so easy. You have to work harder than people who have money in the first place. It's like being stuck in a hole and trying to dig yourself out, but the earth keeps falling in on top of you."

"But we won't stay like this. I won't let us," I told her. "I'll make things better for us."

"I believe you." She smiled back at me. "Together we can make a better life."

Like the one we used to have with Ross at the beginning. The life that should have been so perfect. Except it wasn't.

"Money isn't everything," Mum said. "It doesn't make you happy."

We both knew that was true.

I'm so lost in my thoughts that I don't spot them at first. But then I do. They are difficult to miss.

A tall, skinny figure in a dark jacket, hood up, walking past my house. I stand back, concealed a little by the huge tree at the end of the road. Is it him? It is the same person I saw before? I can't be sure but doubt claws at me. Mum seemed so certain we were safe now. The police had told us that this was it, that he wouldn't find us again, not after the injunction that Mum had taken out.

But what if they were wrong? What if Ross is back?

I realize I'm breathing raggedly. I need to go and speak to this person, find out who they are. It might be nothing at all.

I take a deep breath and lift my head.

But when I look back up – they have gone.

Mum is sitting in the living room, piles of letters spread out in front of her. I know what they are – all the benefit letters and applications. She's been scribbling figures in her notebook and is so absorbed she doesn't notice me come in. The TV is on and Henry is sitting in front of it, munching on a carrot stick. On the floor, Amy is laid out on a blanket playing with a stuffed elephant, kicking her lovely fat legs in the air with excitement.

"Alice!" Henry squeals, jumping up.

I pull him into a hug. "How was school? Did you have loads of fun?"

Henry is in reception at primary school. Unlike me, he seems to have found school to be quite easy.

"Good. Really good. I love it. I've made a best friend called Callum and my teacher has pink hair."

"Pink hair?" I smile. "Wow, that sounds awesome."

I glance over at Mum. A tiny frown is etched on her face and I can see that she is chewing the inside of her cheek again.

"Mum? What's up?"

She looks up, gaze unfocused, and finally sees me. "Hello, love. How was school?" She rises, stretches, and gives me a hug, a smile returning to her face. "You had art today, didn't you?"

"Yeah, that part was great," I say. I glance down at the stacks of letters. "Mum, are you OK?"

"I'm fine." She half laughs. "Just tired – that's

all. I've only just found these letters in Henry's bedroom. I think our boy has been playing postie again."

Henry giggles. "I put the letters into my sack to deliver later, Mummy."

"Your clothes bin is not the post sack, Henry," Mum scolds. "It's just lucky I found them when I was doing the washing. . ."

I pull a face at Henry. He's such a monkey. "So there's nothing wrong?" I ask Mum.

"No. Why would there be?" She takes a step closer. "Alice? Are you OK?" she asks.

"I—"

I want to tell her about the person outside the house. I want to tell her that I'm scared it's Ross, or someone who Ross has paid to watch us. He's done it before. When we left in the past, he's managed to track us down again. Ross always finds a way.

But then I look down at Henry. He is staring up at me, wide-eyed and afraid.

"I – I don't like school," I say instead. "I can't seem to make any friends except Alfie, and he's busy with football all the time."

"Aw, love," Mum says, pulling me into a hug. "I know it's hard, being the new girl again. But you have to go to school and you have to work hard. It's the only way to do well in life."

That's been drummed into me ever since I was a little girl. Work hard, get ahead.

"Yeah – I know."

"Don't stress, Alice. It'll get easier soon. You'll see." She grins. "Remember, you promised to make us all rich one day."

I force a smile back. I hope so much that she is right and this will feel better soon.

And I hope that all my fears are wrong.

Chapter Five

I have one picture of my real dad.

Alfie has hundreds of his mum. They're all round the house or stuffed into albums. He can look at those photos and he can *remember*. He can see his mum in the garden laughing, eyes squinting against the sun, or look her on the beach licking an ice cream, laughing because some of it has got on her nose, or pushing him on a swing, higher and higher. He has all these images mixed in with his own memories and they help to keep her alive. So, in a funny way, I think that he's lucky.

I don't say that to him, of course. But I have one picture and it tells me nothing. The photo is faded slightly, as though it's been bleached by the sun. Mum says it was taken at a house party. My dad is sitting on a sofa and grinning at the person taking the photo; there are a couple of other people squashed next to him but the photo has cut them off. He has a can of beer in his hand and is holding it up to the camera. His mouth is open like he's in the middle of saying cheers. His hair is dark and a bit long and his eyes are also dark, like mine. I can't tell if he's funny, kind or clever. He is just a person at a party, drinking his beer.

"He was older than me. I was seventeen and at college, he was already in his twenties," she said once. "He was cool and popular. I only knew of him because he used to be at some of the house parties I went to."

"So what happened?"

"We got together. Went out a couple of times, nothing serious, but I got pregnant," she said. "By then I realized that I didn't want to be with your dad. He wasn't exactly the reliable type, shall we say, and he certainly wasn't interested in settling down." She squeezed my arm. "So we broke up. We were both young and hardly knew each other, so it was never going to be a perfect mix. I later heard he moved away, which is a shame because he missed out on the best thing that could have happened to him, and that's you."

"Did he know about me?"

"He did, but he had other – well, commitments. To be honest I don't think he could stand the pressure and panicked. I thought it was best for all of us to let him go." She gently lowered her arm and sighed. "Alice, some people just aren't equipped to be good parents or partners. I knew we'd be better without him. I did what was best."

I hope what she said was right, but I wish I could stop thinking about him. I wish I could stop wondering what he's like. But it's like there's a piece missing inside of me.

I don't want to feel this way for ever.

"I can't be your real dad but I can be a good dad" – that was what Ross had said.

At first I believed that. But when we moved back in with him after that first escape, things soon changed. In fact, I don't think anything was ever the same again.

First, it was the arguments. They would wake me up in the night.

And then the bruises appeared.

The first was a bright red mark just under her eye. Mum said she had scratched herself with a bracelet. Then there was a raw patch on her forehead. She blamed this on a low-hanging branch. And then there was a purple bruise on her cheek. This time she had caught herself with the cupboard door.

"You know how clumsy I can be," she laughed. Ross laughed too. But I noticed that her hands were shaking and she couldn't meet my eye.

I realized then. Even though I was only really little, I realized what was happening.

Ross wasn't going to make our life better.

Instead, he was going to make it far, far worse.

*

On Friday, I arrange to meet Alfie by the seafront, opposite the blackened tree that he likes so much. I really don't know why, it gives me the creeps. It's really warm still, even though it's early evening, but there is a light breeze and it catches the fresh tang of salt from the sea. This always helps to clear my mind.

Alfie, as usual, is late. He's always late meeting from football practice. I don't mind. It's lovely to be here in the sun, watching the kids shriek and play in the waves. I imagine I'm out there with them, dipping into the cool water, allowing it to lap at my feet and sting my skin.

So, I've managed a full week at school. A full week of long, boring lessons and crowds of boring people. I'd like to say that the time passed quickly, but I would be lying. The week dragged, as usual. I'm glad it's over now, but the feeling of relief is overtaken by the overwhelming feeling of anxiety that is seeping through me.

"Hey!"

I turn around and see Alfie. He is flushed and

carrying his football.

"Good session?" I ask, smiling.

"Yeah – it was a tough one tonight. The coach was working us extra hard. Fun, though."

"Rather you than me." I tip my head back to the breeze. "Fancy some chips?"

"Always."

We go to our usual van. It's my turn to treat Alfie, he's been paying out for me for ages, but when I reach into my bag for my wallet he shakes his head.

"Don't worry about it. My dad gave me some cash before I left."

"But it's my turn." I don't want Alfie thinking that I have no money all the time – even though it's the truth. My wallet is full of old change. I still hate him knowing this about me. It feels like a weakness somehow.

"It's not a big deal, Alice," he says, and then before I can argue he orders us two big bags of chips. The smell is amazing. My stomach begins to growl like I haven't eaten for months.

We walk back over to the seafront and sit

on the rocks. The sea is out so the beach looks huge. Near the water there are lots of dog walkers trudging through the wet sand.

"We could bring Poppy next time," I say.

Poppy is Alfie's dog and I love her. She's still a puppy and she's the sweetest thing ever. Nobody knows exactly what mix of breeds she is, as Alfie and his dad got her from a rescue centre. Alfie's dad refers to her a "dolly mixture". Whatever mix she is, it's created this long limbed, silky furred and extremely soppy creature. She makes me feel better whenever I'm around her.

"Dad keeps saying it's too soon to bring her to the beach, that she needs proper training, but I reckon she'll be fine." He eats a chip. "He fusses too much. He always thinks the worst is going to happen."

"He just worries," I say. I won't hear a word against Alfie's dad. He's probably the kindest person I've ever met. "It's nice."

Alfie glances over at me. "Are you thinking about your dad again?"

I shrug, dig my toe into the rocks. "I dunno – maybe. I don't know why, he was a waste of space by the sounds of it."

I stare out to sea. It looks so grey today, so murky. "I reckon it'll storm later," Alfie says. His eyes are also on the churning sea.

"You think?"

"Yeah. That's why the weather is so weird. You can feel the pressure pressing down on you all the time." He scoops up some sand and lets it trickle through his fingers. "That's why I like storms. It gets rid of all that horrible, heavy feeling. Everything feels much fresher and brighter after."

"Sounds great," I say. He frowns a little. "You seem down, Alice. Things are better, aren't they? Now that you're in your house."

I rub at the skin around my temples. Alfie is right, the air is so thick and heavy it feels like it's actually pressing against my head. It's not helping me think straight.

"Alice?" he probes.

"It's nothing really." I shift uneasily. "I guess I'm just . . . waiting for something to go wrong, do you know what I mean?"

Alfie shakes his head. "It won't go wrong. Not

this time. Ross has gone. You know that."

I dig my fingers further into the stones.

"I think someone has been watching the house," I say finally.

Alfie sits bolt upright, his dark eyes wide. "Are you serious?"

I shrug. My fingers are still digging, finding the soft sand now. It's cold and grainy against my fingertips. "I've seen someone, a few times. They're wearing a coat with a hood and they just ... watch the house. And then they go away again. Mum doesn't know and I don't want to tell her."

"Do you think it's him?" Alfie asks, his cheeks reddening.

I rub my forehead again. "I don't think so. I've only seen them for a second and I haven't seen their face. But I think they're quite young – not much older than us."

But that doesn't mean Ross isn't involved. Maybe he's using someone else this time. Whenever we've left before, he's always tried to find us. It's never stopped him before.

Alfie is quiet for a moment. I know he's thinking it all through; he doesn't like rushing into anything. He likes facts. He likes to make careful, considered decisions.

"It could be nothing," he says finally. "You're in a new house. A new street. It could be just someone checking you out. Someone nosy."

"I guess," I say.

"But even so, I think you should tell your mum."

I look up, catch his gaze.

"I don't want to worry her, Alfie, she's got enough to think about," I say. "What if it's nothing?"

"Well, if it's nothing, she won't be worried for long, will she?" Alfie reasoned. "But if it's something, then she needs to know. And she needs to know soon."

I walk home. I promised Alfie I'd talk to Mum before I left, but the words felt like a lie as soon as they left my lips.

I know Mum is still worried about money, but

at least she's laughing and joking again. I haven't caught her crying since we moved into the house. And Henry is sleeping through the night again. We're coming back together as a family at last. Things are working out.

So, I could talk to Mum. I could tell her everything and see what kind of storm that creates.

Or. . .

I keep walking, my mind whirring, my thoughts tumbling into place.

Or I could investigate this a little more myself first. I could find out who this person is and why they've been hanging around. After all, it could be nothing.

I can do this on my own.

Chapter Six

The next time we left Ross, we went somewhere called a hostel. It was a special place for women who needed to escape from their partners to go.

When the woman who worked there showed us to our room, she gave Mum a hug.

"He'll leave you alone here," she said. "You're safe."

Mum flushed. "Oh, Ross isn't so bad. I'm not even sure I should be here. He just gets worked up sometimes," she said. "It's my fault. I wind him up. I should know better."

She didn't show the woman the bruises on

her arm where Ross had grabbed her too tightly the night before, but I knew they were there and every time I thought of them a hot feeling built up behind my eyes.

For ages, I blamed Mum for upsetting Ross. I used to think it was her fault for not keeping him happy. But I was beginning to understand now that sometimes nothing could make Ross happy – nothing at all. Last night had been enough to convince me of that.

I watched as she touched her hair in the mirror. It was a small gesture, but I saw her flinch. Ross hadn't liked it when she returned from the hairdresser yesterday.

"You know I like it long," he said. "It suits you so much better."

"But I only took a few inches off – it was getting so ratty." She paused. "I thought you'd like it. I wanted to look good for you."

"It looked beautiful before." Ross sighed with disappointment. "The trouble is – you never listen."

"And neither do you. . ." Mum had whispered back so quietly, but only once he'd left the room.

Only I heard her. We both knew that Ross's quiet, blunt words were laced with ice. She would pay for her mistake later, she always did.

When she woke me up at midnight, her eyes blurry with tears, I could hardly believe we were going again.

"What's different this time?" I whispered.

"He tried to punch my belly," she replied. "I don't think he meant to. I think he forgot. But it's enough."

Mum was four months pregnant with his little boy. I knew if she wasn't going to protect herself, she might at least try to protect him.

The room was small, with two beds squeezed inside. I could hear a woman in the next room sobbing. The place stank of old cigarettes and stale coffee. Mum sat on one of the narrow beds and squeezed her hands together. I could see tears in her eyes, but she didn't cry.

On the bed next to her was her phone.

"I'm not calling him," she said firmly. "And I won't pick up if he calls."

But her eyes couldn't leave it alone, like she expected it to come alive at any second. I kept staring at it too, willing it not to ring, praying that Ross wouldn't call her.

We were in that place for two weeks before Ross came to get us. He was waiting for us at the end of the road in the car.

I should have known. I heard her sobbing in the bathroom the night before. She had rung him and told him where we were. She missed him too much.

Ross grinned at me in the rear-view mirror as he drove us away. He would have tracked us down easily anyway, he said. He would never let his girls go. Or his little boy. His precious little boy.

"We have to stop Mummy doing anything silly like that again, don't we, Alice?" he said. He had reached over and stroked Mum's arm. Her bruises were faded by now.

"It won't happen again," he said softly. "That was the last time. Things will be better now."

But some people can never, ever be trusted.

We learnt that the hard way.

*

It's Saturday and Alfie's dad and I are at the match. I slept badly and keep stifling yawns. I don't want Alfie's dad to think there is anything wrong.

We are standing by the touchline on an uneven and pretty dry pitch. There are loads of parents here gathered together. Some are sitting in little camping chairs and others are standing like us, moving between each other and chatting.

"Tough match, this one," Alfie's dad tells me excitedly. Poppy sees a squirrel and leaps up, and he tugs her gently back and shushes her.

Alfie's team are busy warming up. They are wearing their orange away kit today. Alfie is running up and down on the spot. He grins when he sees us and waves.

"Is Ben not coming?" I ask. Ben usually always comes to Alfie's games; he has the biggest voice out of everyone and always goes mad when he scores.

"No, he's seeing his grandad," Alfie's dad replies. "Nice lad."

"Yeah."

I bunch my hands in my pockets, feeling

oddly disappointed. Ben is loads of fun at the match and though I'd never admit it to Alfie, he can make the game a lot more interesting. He always makes fun of the players for getting too "intense" and worked up and he does a wicked impression of Alfie's uptight manager. It's such a shame he's not here.

The referee has gathered the teams together so I know the game is about to start. I stand more upright, try and look alert. Another yawn dances in my throat but I manage to swallow it back down again.

The referee blows the whistle, some kid from the other team kicks the ball. It's started.

"Come on, son," Alfie's dad shouts. He always does that at the beginning of the game. Poppy whines softly, like she knows something is going on. Even I feel that flutter of anxiety. I never feel like these matches are a big deal. I only come to give Alfie some support, but it's only when I'm here that I realize how much I want him to win.

"Go, Alfie," I say, under my breath. I'm too shy to shout out loud like everyone else here.

It's a fast, tight game, but no one has scored yet. I can hardly keep up with what is going on as the ball moves from end to end. The other team have a chance on goal, but miss. The small gaggle of away fans that are standing on the far side from us groan.

Alfie has the ball. He does one of his fast runs that he is so good at. I can feel the adrenaline pulsing through me as I watch him swerve around one player, and then another. I bounce lightly up and down on the spot.

"C'mon. . ."

He crosses it into the box and one of his teammates, a tall boy with a shock of bright ginger hair, runs to meet it, guiding the ball past the keeper and into the net.

Our side of the crowd explodes into cheers. Alfie's dad squeezes my arm. I look up at him and see the pride burning away in his eyes.

"Did you see that cross, Alice. What a cross!"

"I know. I know. It was amazing."

"He's such a star."

I smile back, trying to ignore the ache inside

of me. What must it be like to have a dad who loves you as much as this?

I quickly look away again. I can feel tears building. I don't want to make a fool of myself here. I concentrate on Alfie instead, who is hugging the goal scorer. He then turns to us and pumps his fist. He is glowing with happiness. The whistle blows. It's over.

I wave back. "Well done," I croak. Even though I know he can't hear me. "Well done!"

My eyes scan the crowd behind him, the away fans. They are standing quiet and sullen. I guess they are feeling pretty fed up at the moment. But then my eyes fall on a figure standing at the edge of the crowd. He's leaning on a battered-looking bike and wearing a dark hoodie, which is odd in this warm weather.

I swear he's staring straight at me.

I turn back to Alfie's dad, wondering if I should say something, but he is already in deep conversation with another parent next to him. And then I turn back and the figure is gone.

*

"Why do you keep looking out of your window?"

I jump as Henry comes up behind me. He is clutching his favourite toy car in his hand. He drops it on my bed and settles himself down beside me. "You keeping looking out there. Are you looking for something?"

"No," I say. "I just like being nosy, that's all . . . seeing what the neighbours are all up to."

The lie trips easily off my tongue.

My eyes continue to scan the street in front of me. It's a bit compulsive now. I've been watching the neighbours come and go for the last hour or so. I've seen the older kids playing hide-and-seek by the tree and a couple of women having a chat on the corner. But so far there has been no sign of the loitering figure from before.

Maybe I am overthinking it. After all, there were so many boys wearing hoodies at the game today. It was probably an older brother of one of the players. I am being an idiot and worrying over nothing. Again.

Henry thumps my arm lightly.

"What are you looking for?" He wipes his

nose. He seems to have another cold already. "Is it something exciting?"

"Father Christmas," I say, with a grin.

"You can't look for him now. It's April, silly," he tells me matter-of-factly. "Father Christmas will be on holiday. Somewhere like Bognor. Mum told me he needs a rest too."

Bognor is the only holiday place Henry knows because it's the only place we've been on holiday – a week-long caravan stay when we left Ross the third time. A woman at the refuge owned a van on the caravan site. It was the best holiday ever – just the three of us, by the sea, not worrying for once. But when the week was over, there was Ross, ready to pick us up.

"Call this a holiday?" he had said, looking around the caravan park. "We'll go somewhere better next holiday. America or Spain, how would you like that, Alice?"

But I knew by then we wouldn't ever go on holiday. Ross didn't like us leaving the house. He said he liked us all together where he could keep an eye on things.

"I'm sure Santa is busy making sandcastles somewhere," I reply now. "Even in this weather."

"Are you sad?" Henry asks, pressing his tiny body against mine.

I pull away from the window and turn towards him. "No, not at all," I say, surprised. "Why do you think I'm sad?"

"You seem sad, that's all. And you keep looking out of the window."

"I'm fine," I tell him, ruffling his hair. "I just like to keep an eye on things, just in case."

"Just in case what?" His body stiffens a little.

I shrug. "Just in case – nothing."

Henry used to have bad dreams. Mum called them *night terrors*. He would scream in the night and sit up in bed, saying that he could see things crawling up the walls. Sometimes he would wet himself or bang his head against the wall.

Mum said it was from all the stress that Ross caused. I never really knew how much Henry understood. I never thought all the fighting, the moving, the upset had affected him. I assumed he was too young to be bothered by it all, but now I look into his eyes and know that wasn't true.

"We are safe now," I tell him. "This is a lovely house. A safe house. There's nothing to worry about now."

"You promise?" His eyes are wide, watching me.

I nod, but I don't speak. I don't want to be another person who lies easily to him. Like Ross did to us so many times before.

I'm not that person.

I'm doing my homework at the kitchen table. Alfie's old table.

Amy is asleep in her cot and Henry is splashing in the bath upstairs, while Mum attempts to scrub him down. I honestly can't see the point in most of the stuff we learn. When am I ever going to need the circumference of a circle? Seriously?

At my last school, the teachers were concerned that I was "falling behind". They called Mum into a meeting and everything. They told her I had "potential", but my concentration levels were poor and I lacked focus. And then my new school called me in for playing truant. Mum gave me a lecture that time. Said I had to start knuckling down.

I sigh and push the maths homework away from me.

I'm still hungry after our dinner. Mum's portion sizes are getting smaller and smaller. I don't think she ate anything herself either.

I open the fridge. It's a pretty depressing sight. Some slices of ham, a lump of cheese and Henry's favourite yoghurts. I shut the door. Maybe, I think, I should invite myself back to Alfie's for tea one night next week. His dad cooks the most amazing food – he could keep me full for a week. And then there would be more for the others.

But I don't want to keep relying on Alfie. If he gets signed, he'll be away anyway.

It could change his life.

It could change everything.

Something tugs in my stomach that isn't just hunger, and I cross my arms over it in an attempt to suppress the feeling.

I wander back into the living room. Upstairs I can hear Mum's gentle voice as she reads Henry's bedroom story. He is giggling as she does all the silly voices. She used to do that to me when I was really little. I used to love snuggling up next to her and letting myself be swept up the worlds she was telling me about. "The Three Little Pigs" used to be my favourite. I loved it when she did the scary voice of the wolf:

"Then I'll huff and I'll puff and I'll blow your house down. . ."

She was different then. Before Ross. I can still hear her confident voice reading it to me, her laugh ringing out. She even laughed different then.

And then of course it all changed. Ross came and swept us away into a new life. Soon I was settled into my big new bed in my pretty new bedroom. Mum was relaxed and happy, but not for long.

Ross seemed like a nice man who kept us safe.

But we were so wrong. In actual fact we were like the three little pigs. We thought we were safe and cosy in our lovely little house. We thought we had the house made of bricks, so sturdy and strong it could withstand anything. We thought we had kept the wolves safely locked away. Nothing bad could ever get to us.

But of course we didn't realize that the wolf was living with us all the time.

And one day he blew everything away.

Chapter Seven

After Henry was born, the days blurred into one. There were good times and bad times. The bad times were very similar – loud words behind closed doors, broken plates, hidden sobs. I got used to seeing Mum dress in long-sleeved tops to hide the marks on her arms where Ross grabbed and pinched her. I got used to the heavy make-up she wore to hide the bruises on her face. I got used to seeing her with her hair hanging down, thick and glossy – just like Ross liked, with not a hair out of place.

My mum was turning into a character I barely

recognized, but I accepted it because we were happy, right? We had our lovely house. I had all the toys and clothes I could ever want. We had Henry now. Beautiful, bubbly Henry.

It was worth it, wasn't it? This life was worth some painful moments.

But one night was different from the rest. It's one I've never forgotten.

Henry was about a year old, so I must've been about ten. I'd started having nightmares and I was too scared to go to sleep. So I went downstairs to get Mum. I just wanted her to tell me everything would be OK.

It wasn't that late, but Mum was still up. I knew she had had trouble sleeping because Henry had been really ill with croup that week. This had made both her and Ross grumpy. They still had the TV on, and it was really loud. I remember thinking the shouting and crying was coming from the telly.

It was only when I pushed open the door that I realized that the noise was coming from Mum. I'd never heard her cry out so loudly before. Ross turned as I stepped into the room. His face was completely different to anything I'd ever seen. It was all twisted and ugly. It was a mask that turned my body to liquid.

"Mum. . ." I whispered.

He had Mum by the hair and was pulling her back towards him. Her face was white with pain, her scalp red raw where the hair was being ripped back.

"Go!" Ross hissed. "Back to bed. Now! Go!"

And I did. I ran up the stairs and jumped back into my bed. I pulled my duvet over my head and lay there shaking.

I didn't move, not for hours. I lay there humming, trying not to hear the sounds from downstairs and trying desperately to forget Ross's face.

I was no longer scared of nightmares.

Because nothing would ever be as scary as what I'd just seen.

It's Monday and I haven't seen the figure again – not since the game, if it was them at all.

I need to get a grip, I think. Whatever that was, it was probably all in my head.

Mum kisses me lightly on the cheek as I go to leave for school. I notice that she has her Messenger up and is obviously chatting to someone.

"Who's that?" I ask.

She turns it over quickly. "No one. Just organizing a boiler check."

It didn't look like that though. It looked like she'd been having a long chat with someone. I frown.

"Why won't you tell me who it is?" I say uneasily.

"Because it's nothing, honestly. You need to stop worrying so much." She hands me a fiver for lunch money. "Off you go, you'll be late."

"OK," I say. "Thanks."

The smile returns to her face as quickly as it disappeared. "You have nothing to worry about, Alice. Honestly."

But if she's chatting to Ross again, I have every reason to worry.

All the way to school, the same thought echoes around my head – the wolf could be back. He could be pacing outside right now waiting for the right time to strike. He could destroy everything that we have managed to build. After all, he's done it so many times before, wormed his way back into Mum's heart with his stupid excuses and weak lies. And she falls for it.

Every. Single. Time.

This is what Ross does. This is why people like him when they first meet him. He seems so kind and charming and funny – you can't not want to be around him. It's why I cried myself to sleep the first time we left him. I *missed* him. Despite the fact that I knew he was doing bad things. He would always say things that made it seem OK afterwards.

All adults fight, Alice.

Your mum – she can be difficult sometimes. It's hard to keep her happy. I'm only ever trying to do right by her.

I love you all so much. I'll never do anything to hurt you again.

I'm not the baddie here, Alice. You know that.

As I make my way towards the main entrance I see Chloe and Esme sitting on the steps.

"Hey!" Chloe says as I approach, and flashes me a bright smile.

"Hi," I say as casually as possible. I shift the bulky rucksack on to my other shoulder. I see Chloe's eyes graze my body. God how I hate my shoes.

As though she can read my mind, Chloe's eyes linger on my feet. I see that tiny, snake-like smile appear on her lips and then it is gone – almost like it was never there at all. I could almost convince myself that I'd imagined it.

"How's the new house?" Esme asks sweetly.

"It's all good," I say, keeping my voice level. Just waiting for the comeback. It doesn't take long.

"You're on the Cranbrooke estate, aren't you?" Esme says.

"Yeah, that's right."

She sniffs. "Might wanna make sure you keep your valuables locked up then."

"If you have any," Chloe adds smoothly, then she holds out her hands. "No offence. I'm just saying. . ."

"Just saying" and "it's only banter" are Chloe and Esme's favourite things to say. They use it as some kind of defence to say really nasty things and then act as if it is just one big joke. Except it's not. It never is.

"Things are a little tight at the minute," I say, through gritted teeth. "We've just moved house. My mum needs to get a job."

Seriously? Why am I justifying myself to these two? I should just walk on by. Ignore them. Get on with my life. But I don't. Something is holding me back.

"Oh, I totally get it," Chloe says, her expression serious. She lowers her voice. "When we moved to our new house last year, money was a problem. Dad wouldn't let us order takeaways for weeks. He cut way back on my clothing allowance."

I stared at her. Was she for real?

"That sounds tough," Esme says sympathetically.

"Yeah – really tough," I mutter.

Try not having hot water for a week, I think.

"It *was* hard," Chloe says. "I know what it's like."

In the distance the school bell rings, and my stomach lurches in response. I am both relieved to get away and anxious about another day in the building. The school day suddenly seems so long and looming.

"I can't wait to see what you wear on Friday, Alice," Esme says as she gets up from the step. "It's bound to be something really quirky."

"What do you mean?" I ask, confused.

"Oh, didn't you know?" She smiles back. "It's non-uniform day. It's a chance for you to come into school wearing your best clothes. Stand out. We can really check out your *style* then."

Her smile is fixed and cool. I know exactly what she is saying here.

You don't have any best clothes.

You don't have any style.

You are going to stand out for all the wrong reasons.

And she is totally right.

They move to walk off. Chloe turns back

suddenly, her hair swishing. "I almost forgot to tell you, Alice. There was a kid hanging around outside the school the other day. He was asking people if they knew you."

I swallow. "Who was he?"

"Oh, I dunno. Some boy – youngish." She sniggers. "Not much to look at. Bit of state really. But he wanted to know if you came to this school."

"And you told him I did?"

She shrugs. "Sure. Why not? It's not a big deal, is it?" I don't say anything and she flushes.

"He said he knew you. He said he was your family."

"Anything else?" I ask.

"He asked where you lived," she says, a bit more defensively now, "and I said I didn't know but I told him the estate. I said you sometimes go and watch the matches on the weekend."

I think of the boy on the bike last Saturday and my skin prickles.

"Did I do something wrong?" she asks.

Maybe nothing, I think. Or maybe she's just ruined everything.

Chapter Eight

After that night when I saw Ross pull Mum's hair back, things were suddenly as they were before.

It didn't help that Henry was so much closer to Mum. He only really liked it when she held him and often got upset if she wasn't there, or put him down for too long. Mum didn't mind. But Ross was sulky about it.

"Why is he such a mummy's boy?" I heard Ross hiss at her in the kitchen. "He's always clinging on to you. Crying and sobbing. It's not healthy being like that."

"He's just used to me, that's all. I'm home all

the time," Mum soothed. "After he was ill, he wants his mummy."

"You make him like that," Ross said. "You'll end up turning him into a wet little kid. You ruin everything."

It didn't help that Henry seemed to react to Ross's mood. He started to cry every time Ross went to pick him up.

"I won't bother then," Ross would say coldly, before storming out of the room. "The little brat can have no dad – like his sister."

His words cut through me like a knife. I froze on the spot, but Ross only smirked when he saw me.

"What do you expect, Alice? You're no better. A proper little mummy's girl. You only love me when you want something."

That wasn't true and he knew it, but it still hurt. I ran to my room in tears and heard him sniggering behind me. It was the first time he'd been directly cruel to me.

Later still I heard his cold words screaming at Mum as he blamed her for ruining everything, for destroying the good life that they had. He said that she had made her kids "turn on him", that she was "ungrateful" and "evil". What was worse than those words were the sounds of Mum's quiet sobs coming back. I knew he was hurting her again, I knew his fists were flying, and there was nothing I could do to stop it.

As much as Ross tried to fight, he couldn't keep that side of him locked away for ever. It was always going to come back. We were the fools for not realizing sooner.

As I walk to maths, I wonder who the boy might be and if he's someone Ross has sent after us. Ross has loads of family – brothers and sisters and therefore lots of nephews and nieces, they came over for family parties and stuff. I can think of a few boys who were a bit older than me. There was one who was always hanging around Ross, looking up to him like he was some kind of god. What was his name?

Billy. That's it. Billy with the slightly crooked teeth and blond hair.

It would be just like Ross to send one of his lot out to find us.

I walk into class and settle myself down. I take some calming breaths like Mum taught me to do when I get wound up. I can feel my body slowly start to unwind. I unclench my fists.

This might not be so bad. If Ross has sent Billy, then I can speak to him. Reason with him. Scare him off, if I have to.

I close my eyes for a second and let a tiny smile rest on my face.

If Ross thinks he's going to frighten me, he's wrong. I don't scare that easy.

He taught me that himself.

Alfie waves me over to his table at lunch. I hesitate – he's with Ben, and I wonder if he'll want me around. But Ben is waving too, so I go.

To be fair, I do quite like sitting with them. For popular boys they aren't mean, or at least I don't think they are. Ben is cool and dead funny, you can kind of relax around him. Today he has a streak of yellow in his hair and his eyebrow is still very much shaved off.

"The canary look is in right now, apparently," Alfie says to me, grinning.

Ben sits back on his seat, grinning lazily. "You're just jealous because I stand out," he replies. "People are scared of 'different', it makes them feel uneasy. It makes them question how boring they are. Right, Alice?"

"I like the hair," I say. "I still can't say I understand the eyebrow."

He touches his eyebrow. "Oh yeah – that. I never should've used my mum's Bic. It was dead blunt."

"Seriously, I wonder why I hang around with you," Alfie says. "You look lopsided."

"Every day is interesting – that's why. And you've got the lovely Alice here for balance and sanity." He waves a hand in my direction and smiles. I suddenly realize his eyes are very blue and his smile lights up his entire face, it's so fresh and genuine.

Despite myself I blush. I don't think a boy has ever called me "lovely" before. Ben winks.

"Yeah, she's super sane," Alfie teases. "Doesn't see stalkers on every street corner."

"Alfie!" I hiss. He flushes up and I know it was an accident.

"Sorry," he murmurs. "I wasn't thinking. But it wouldn't be a bad thing to talk to Ben about it, you know. He might have some ideas."

Ben leans forward, interested. "What's this?"

"It's nothing," I say, glaring at Alfie.

"You can scowl at me all you want," says Alfie. "But I think if you're worried you should tell people."

"Fine," I snap. "Ben, someone's been watching my house. And then last week, came to the school and asked about me. Chloe of all people decided to be helpful and more or less gave out my address." I shake my head. "Then he showed up at Alfie's football game on Saturday where she also told him I'd be. I don't know why she didn't just give out my bank details to be done with it."

"Well, to be fair, she wouldn't have your bank details," Ben says dryly, but his eyes are fixed on mine. For once he doesn't seem to be joking around. "And that's the same kid who was outside your house?"

"I guess so," I say. "Can't be a coincidence, can it?"

"I guess not..." Ben says, sounding a little uncertain.

Alfie shakes his head. "I'm sorry, Alice, I didn't take it seriously."

I smile at him, all my anger gone. He's right; it's a relief to talk about it.

"That's OK."

"Do you know who it might be?"

I take a deep breath. I haven't told Ben about Ross, only Alfie, but I think he's probably figured out that something isn't right with our past. I tell them my suspicions about Ross and Billy and they both nod as I talk.

"You need to tell your mum, like I told you," Alfie says. "And probably someone at school."

"I dunno." I take a sip of my drink. "Then the police will get involved again."

"Yeah," says Alfie grimly. "As they should be. Tell your mum, Alice. She'll want to know."

"The thing is..." I hesitate. This is somehow the most difficult thing to tell them. "She's been texting someone. It might be him." I glance up at them both. "She's – she's done this in the past," I explain. "Got back in touch with him, gone back to him. I don't know if I can trust her."

"You thought this before, though," Alfie reminds me. "Remember?"

I nod. Once I'd seen a police car outside our house. I was sure that Mum had gone back to Ross. But I had got it all wrong. The police had come to tell us Ross had been arrested.

But Mum has broken my trust so much in the past. How can I trust her again?

"I still don't want to worry her. Not yet," I say. "It could be nothing. I need to figure this out on my own."

"Not on your own," Ben says. "You've got us." He glances at Alfie, who is grinning. "Right, mate?"

Alfie nods. "Yeah – of course you've got us. You've always got us."

*

It is the end of the day but I can't face the chaos outside, with everyone else clamouring and shrieking to get out of school, so I escape to the art room again for a little while. I'm relieved to be out of the crowded corridors and once again in this quiet, cool space.

I need to think. I go to the art studio, hoping Ms Monroe will be there and I can sit quietly for a bit.

She's there, filling in some paperwork. She gives me a smile and a wave. There is only one other girl in here. I recognize her from my year – Lauren – she also must be here just to catch up on work or something. She's in my English class, but never talks to me. She's one of those people who keep themselves to themselves. She always looks good though and her bag is a designer one – so I'm guessing she's from the posher end of town, like Chloe and Esme. I get my sketchbook out of my tray and sit at the back by the window. Lauren glances up at me, seems to notice someone is here for the first time, then goes back to her work. I try not to stare but I can see the piece she is doing from here – it's of a face and it's amazing. She is obviously really talented.

I pick up a pencil. I try not to think too much this time. I just allow myself to draw, loving the scratchy sound of lead against the sheet. I can feel my entire body uncurling. My spine is no longer stiff but feels like elastic. I lean over the desk, resting my head on my arm.

I don't hear Ms Monroe approach.

"Alice – that's beautiful," she says. "It's such a powerful image. You really need to come to my group on Wednesday. You are so good."

I blink. "Thanks," I say.

"Who is it?" she asks.

I look at the picture. I hadn't been aware that I had been drawing anyone in particular, but now I can see it quite clearly. The high cheekbones, the sweep of hair moving into a quiff at the top, the teasing eyes that sparkle.

I have drawn Ben.

Chapter Nine

The next time we left Ross, we went to a B & B. The smell there was of fried food and stale smoke.

Mum's friend Wendy had told her to go there. Mum had once had lots of friends but Ross didn't like them and gradually she stopped seeing them. But Wendy was a mum at the school; she was tall with a wide smile and a loud voice and she would always hug Mum tight when she saw her. I don't think Ross knew about Wendy.

One time I came in and Mum was sitting on the large double bed with her purse open. All around her on the duvet were piles of paper and coins and one twenty-pound note. Wendy was sitting beside her, an arm around her shoulders.

"Twenty-three pounds and eighty pence." Mum laughed softly. "That's all we have left."

"Nothing in the bank? Didn't you say you had a secret account?"

Mum had done that before, taken money from the machine and kept it somewhere safe. She called it her "emergency funds". It was what she had used to get away from Ross before.

"He knows about that now," she said flatly. "He has my card. It isn't here. He's taken it. He already has the rest of my money."

I saw her shoulders slump. Her entire body seemed to sag inwards. I'd never seen Mum cry.

"I can lend you some more cash," said Wendy. "And there's benefits—"

"But then what?" Mum said. "What about the month after that and the month after that? Always running, always a room somewhere, never knowing where the next month's rent is coming from. It's no way to live for the kids. There's nowhere to go," she whispered. "He always knows how to trap me."

Her hand fell on her stomach. Without saying another word, I knew she was worried about the new baby that grew inside there.

Her gaze was fixed on the wall and it was blank and hopeless. "He'll never let us go."

Lauren leaves the art studio before me. I watch as she packs up her things and moves to the front of the room. She speaks briefly to Ms Monroe. Then, at the doorway, she glances back at me. She doesn't smile – but nods instead. A small acknowledgement that I'm there. Then she is gone.

I start to gather my stuff too. I hadn't realized how late it had got. I need to get home and give Mum a hand.

"Thanks," I say awkwardly when I reach Ms Monroe's desk. "I'll head off too."

She smiles at me and sets down her pen. "You look tired, Alice. Is everything OK? I know things were hard at the beginning, making friends." A strand of her dark hair falls in front of her face and she pushes it back. "And it's great you've got Alfie. That's why I was wondering about the art class, lots of the kids come. Lauren comes along – she's a lovely girl."

"Lauren?" I laugh and say without thinking, "I don't think someone like Lauren would hang around with me."

"I'm sure she would," says Ms Monroe. "If you tried to get to know her. . ."

"No disrespect, miss. But I don't need your help making friends," I mutter.

"Well, if you're—"

"I'm sure," I finish for her.

She nods. "Fair enough. But Alice, please consider coming along on Wednesday. I think you'll enjoy it."

I shrug. "Maybe. . ."

I walk out of the room, holding the picture of Ben. As soon as I'm outside, I scrunch it up in a ball and throw it into the nearest bin.

I approach our street slowly, keeping an eye out for a hooded figure, but no one's there.

The front door of our house is open and Henry is playing on the patch of green with another little boy and an older-looking girl – he waves as I approach.

"Alice! Alice! Look, I've made new friends."

I smile at them. "Hello."

The girl grins back, showing the gaps between her teeth. "I'm Lottie and this is my brother Sam. That's my dad over there."

Sam looks up at me. He has a serious, chubby face and a thick thatch of dark hair. He doesn't say anything. A cheerful-looking man in the garden across the street gives me a wave. So we were wrong. It isn't just old people living around here!

"I'm watching them like a hawk!" he calls.

"Lottie is my new best friend," Henry tells me. "She's eight and has two scooters."

"Wow," I say.

"Have you been out here long?"

Henry squints up his face, thinking about it. "Not long. Mum just went inside to get Amy's dinner on."

"Has anyone walked past here? Anyone come to the house?" I ask Henry.

He's distracted, kicking his ball against the wall. "Erm – no – I dunno."

"I saw someone this morning," Lottie says suddenly. She grins. "I've been watching your house. I want to be a detective when I grow up and detectives always watch for new people in an area."

"OK," I say, laughing. "But who did you see?"

"It was a boy, I think. He put something in your letter box." Her eyes light up for a second. "Is it a present?"

"No—" I say, swallowing. "No. I don't think so."

There is nothing on the doormat when I walk in. Mum must have picked it up, whatever it is.

I pause in the kitchen doorway, watching Mum. She is feeding Amy in the high chair and murmuring into her phone, and as I watch she hangs up. There is still a smell in this house, I swear. OK, Amy's food is overtaking it, but I can still smell the stale cabbages, something rotten.

Mum looks good today, really good. She's brushed her hair loose. I look closely. I think she's wearing eyeliner and a bit of blusher.

Ross always liked her to wear make-up. I don't think she's worn any since.

I look down at the table and see her phone is sitting there, never far out of reach.

Amy pumps her little fists and garbles loudly when I walk in. I gently ruffle her soft hair and plant a kiss on her head. She smells of baby shampoo and the fruit puree stuff that Mum is feeding her.

"Hello, love," Mum says, stirring Amy's soggy food mixture in the bowl. "You're a bit late again. All OK at school?"

"I stayed back and did some more artwork."

Mum's face brightens. "Oh – that's lovely. Hopefully you can bring some home to me soon. We could use a bit of art to brighten the place up."

When I was little Mum used to stick my artwork everywhere. She used to say that it made her feel happy to have my pictures around her. Over time that stopped. Ross used to say that his house wasn't a "bloody art gallery" and he wanted a home, not a nursery. The pictures came down slowly. In the end, the only things that hung on the walls were Ross's photos and expensive paintings.

"It'll be nice to stick some up, alongside Henry's," Mum says. She nods towards the fridge.

There is some artwork there that Henry has obviously done at playschool. I walk over to have a look. One is of a crooked-looking house. I'm pretty sure it's this house. The front door is the same colour.

The other picture is a family. A mum – tall, squiggly blonde hair, a girl – long messy hair, a little boy, and a baby holding a rattle. It's us. Henry has drawn himself with a slightly oversized head and the biggest smile I've ever seen. Above it, in large wonky words, he has written – "FAMLEE".

It's only when I look closely that I can see another figure, taller, standing next to Mum. Henry has obviously rubbed it out but you can still see the faded lines, the dent in the paper where he pressed too hard. A ghost, standing behind us. Despite myself, I shiver.

I turn back to Mum. "You look nice today," I say.

I'm sure I see her cheeks redden. "Oh – oh, thank you, love."

"Did you go out or something?"

"Oh no. I just fancied sprucing myself up a bit today, that's all."

She is looking at Amy, concentrating on her, but I see her bite her lip.

"Who was it on the phone just now?" I'm pushing it, I know. This is none of my business.

"No one. It was just a sales call."

"Mum – did we get something through the door today?" I ask lightly.

Mum pauses for a second. The spoon is midway between the bowl and Amy's mouth.

"No." She turns to look at me. "Why do you ask?"

I shrug, trying to act casual. "Henry's new friend, Lottie, said she saw a boy push something through the door."

"Oh!" Mum seems to relax. "A load of flyers came through this afternoon. You know. For those pizza places in town and a taxi firm, I think. Nothing interesting. I just stuffed them all in the bin."

"But she said she saw him deliver it this morning."

Mum frowns. "What is this, Alice? Why am I getting the third degree over a pizza flyer?"

"I'm only asking if something came through the door."

"And I told you – some flyers did." Mum glares at me. "I didn't look through them. Maybe I missed it. Honestly, Alice, what's going on?"

I glance at the bin. "Is it still in there?"

"If you go rooting through that, you'll put your hand on a load of Amy's food that I chucked on top. Little madam wouldn't eat the first jar I gave her. It's gone, Alice. Just forget about it." She shakes her head. "No one hand delivers anything important nowadays."

"I guess. . ."

But I look back at her. I look at her freshly

made-up face. I look at the phone sitting there by her outstretched hand. I look at wide, outraged eyes.

She's lying to me. I know it.

Ross is back.

She's been talking to him on the phone. She's been listening to his lies again. Taking his letters.

Mum will do what she always does.

She'll let him back in.

Chapter Ten

One time, Ross took me and Henry out together. He didn't do that often. He was always so busy with work or off down the gym, but he said he wanted to spend some time alone with the two of us.

Mum was by then heavily pregnant with Amy. Her stomach was like a huge distended ball that seemed to be weighing her down more and more each day.

One morning, Ross had taken her hand and looked at her sadly.

"You look a mess," he said. He was speaking

so softly I could hardly hear. "It's sad to see. You used to look so beautiful."

Mum flushed and shifted on the spot.

"I'm just tired, that's all – this pregnancy..." she started to say, but Ross put his hand up to stop her.

"Don't! I don't want to hear it," he said gently. He reached into his wallet and drew out some notes. All folded neatly as always. He pressed them into her hand. "Take this. Go to the hairdresser. Get yourself sorted out. Get your hair done how I like it."

"I – I don't know, Ross. I'm so tired – and the kids—"

"I insist." His voice was firmer. "I'll sort the kids out. It's important that you look after yourself, you know. I *like* you to take care of yourself."

She nodded. "Thank you," she said quietly. "I don't know what I'd do without you."

Ross took me and Henry to a nearby burger bar. It was fun. He treated us to giant milkshakes with cream and all the toppings. The young girl behind the till seemed to like Ross. She giggled when he cracked a joke about her bright hair dye and blushed when he winked at her once our food was ready.

"Always have a smile on your face, Alice," he said, when he sat back down again. "It makes people feel good. It'll make you feel good."

Ross always seemed to have that way with people. He could be so charming, so nice. To be honest it was totally confusing.

And I tried. I really did try.

"I don't think all this speculation is helping," says Alfie. "You won't know anything for sure till you speak to your mum."

"Exactly. She might not even be talking to this Ross guy..." Ben points out, waving his pasta-laden fork towards me. "It could be a friend or family."

It's lunchtime and I'm getting the full lecture. *At least they care*, I think. It makes me feel warm inside.

"Mum stopped speaking to most of her friends," I say. "And she doesn't have family."

"What, no one at all?" Ben frowns. "Everyone has *some* family."

"No one," I repeat. "Her mum left when she was a baby. Her dad brought her up and he died when she was in her teens. She lived with foster carers." I push my lunch aside, suddenly not hungry. "She doesn't like talking about it much."

"What about your dad?" Alfie asks. "Does she ever talk to him?"

"No way," I say. "She hasn't seen him since before I was born. She has no clue where he is now."

Ben nods slowly. "So in theory he could be here?"

I shake my head. "It won't be anything to do with him. He ran off to Brighton or somewhere just after Mum found out she was pregnant. She never heard from him again."

"But he might try and make contact?"

"Mum would never have told him where we live. She wouldn't risk it after Ross and she'd talk to me first." I shake my head again. "This is Ross, I just know it."

"Then you need to talk to her," Alfie says matter-of-factly. "It's the only way. I mean, believe me, I hate getting into 'chats' with my dad, but sometimes you have to – don't you?"

"My mum actually enjoys them. She thinks they are bonding or something," Ben says happily. "I think she secretly loves it when I have some kind of crisis. She's totally weird though."

I bite my lip. "I think we've had enough crises for a lifetime in our family."

"Sorry," says Ben.

Alfie gives me a sympathetic smile. "You just need to find out one way or another," he says. He's always so sensible about everything, it's annoying. "There's bound to be a reasonable explanation for all of this. Your mum wouldn't give up everything you fought for. You know that, don't you?"

"Maybe. . ." I admit. "But what about this boy—"

"Maybe you have an admirer," Ben says.

I laugh. "Don't be daft."

"Boys do stupid things when they fancy someone. My dad once tried to shin up a pylon to tie up a message declaring his love for my mum."

"Did he do it?" I ask, grinning.

"Yeah. But then he slipped on the way down and hurt his ankle."

"Well, I haven't got an admirer," I say firmly.

"Either way this kid has your number and your address," Ben points out helpfully.

"Thanks to Chloe," I say, bitterly. I look over at her and Esme, sitting in the centre of the hall as usual, laughing loudly. "I wouldn't even have this problem if Chloe hadn't told him everything."

"It was probably an accident," Alfie says. "They always seem OK."

I sigh. Alfie is good-looking and popular and great at football. He's practically school royalty. He wouldn't understand.

"Sure, they *seem* OK," I say. "And of course they're nice to you. Because you're you and I'm me."

Then I remember our last conversation and groan.

"What's wrong?" Ben asks.

"It's non-uniform day tomorrow."

"So?" Both boys look at me, confused.

"So. I'm going to be wearing the most uncool, tattiest clothes out of everyone and those two" – I glare at their table again – "will be sure to notice."

"I can lend you a football top?" Alfie says helpfully, and I laugh.

"Thanks, but I don't think I can pull it off as well as you. You can sit with me at lunch and cheer me up."

"Aw, Alice, I can't tomorrow," he says apologetically. "I've promised to help Mr Simpson out with some football training."

"I'm free to meet up," Ben says. "Since Alfie is ditching us for football again."

"OK, cool," I say, suddenly feeling self-conscious. "If you're sure."

"It's a date then," he replies. Then his cheeks blaze red. "Not a *date* date. You know what I mean."

I roll my eyes at him.

"It's just lunch," I say. "No big deal."

He smiles back. "Yeah. No big deal."

So why doesn't it feel that way?

*

I ditch art and leave early. I can't face Ms Monroe being nice and asking me questions again.

Making friends when you move all the time is weird. My last school, before we moved to this town, was bigger than this one. Mum tried to get me to join groups and to become part of it all, but I never saw the point. We were living in another hostel and I knew we wouldn't be there long. What was the point of trying to settle in?

There had been one girl, Molly. She was nice. We swapped numbers. We messaged each other in the evening and sometimes I'd go over to her house. It was messy and chaotic, but I loved it. I thought it was what homes were meant to be like.

But then I stopped going. I stopped messaging Molly and I avoided her at school. I couldn't explain it to anyone, not even Mum. I just knew there was no point making a close friend.

And within weeks I was proven right. Ross turned up at the doorstep again – a soppy smile on his face and a bunch of flowers in his hand.

Except this time, when Mum went back to him she didn't look happy about it. She looked defeated, like a mouse that had just been caught by a cat.

And I saw something else in her too.

Anger.

I don't realize how fast I'm walking until I look around me and realize that I'm at the end of the main street and near the turning to the stream. I'm actually out of breath.

I turn, ready to walk down the ragged path alongside the waterway, when something makes me turn and look over my shoulder. And I see him. Tall, skinny. The same blue bike. The same dark hoodie. My breath catches.

Without thinking I shout.

"Hey!"

He lifts his head. It's difficult to see his face from here, but I can see him duck his head. He turns his bike quickly.

"Hey!" I shout again, and start to run after him. "Stop!" I yell.

"I just want to talk to you."

But he is back on his bike and before I know it, he has turned down one of the side streets and gone.

I stop, bend over double and try to regain my breath.

If this boy is Billy and has been sent by Ross – then why won't he talk to me? What is he gaining by just watching me?

Chapter Eleven

Our last months at Ross's were the very worst. Mum had changed, he said. He didn't like it. He blamed Amy. He said the new baby was making her tired and ugly. If Henry left his toys out, he would have to apologize or go without dinner. He would glare at me for even daring to speak. He looked at me like I smelt bad, and that look cut deeper than any knife. If we left a thing out of place he would haul us in and make us tell him what we'd done wrong. Sometimes I didn't even know – it might be a cushion that wasn't straight, a cup left out. The house might've been large and posh and full of nice things – but it was the coldest place I'd ever been in.

One morning I was in the kitchen making toast and he came in. He saw a few toast crumbs on the countertop and his entire body stiffened.

"You spoilt brat," he said, very softly.

"I'm sorry."

Without thinking, I brushed the crumbs on to the floor.

Ross stood there for a second not saying anything, then a slow, cruel smile slipped across his face.

"I shouldn't expect any better really, should I?" he said. "Look at the state of you. You've been dragged up all your life. So you can't really help it, can you?" He took a step closer and I could see the wrinkles in his tanned face, the little chip on his front tooth. "So much like your mum. A complete mess. No hope at all. I feel sorry for you." He clicked his tongue. "I feel sorry for all of you."

And then he walked out, chuckling softly under his breath.

I ground those toast crumbs into his stupid polished tiles and told myself not to cry.

The next morning, I look at my wardrobe and the feeling of dread washes over me once again. There is nothing here. Not really. Nothing that will pass as remotely "fashionable" in the eyes of people like Chloe and Esme.

I have two "nice" dresses that Mum struggled to pay for. One for my leavers disco at primary school, so it's already too small and babyish. It's bright pink with a white collar. If I wear this, I will be lynched.

The other dress is OK – a plain black one that Mum found in a charity shop recently. It's a bit long and there's a small hole by the hem. But it's not too bad.

Other options are my jeans – three pairs, one bought when we were at Ross's that are nice but now comically short, another that is wearing thin on the bum (not a great look), and the final pair are from a charity shop, worn and too baggy. I have quite a few tops that I can wear, but nothing that will make me anything other than a huge fashion mistake.

I finally decide on the second-hand jeans and a plain blue top that used to be Mum's. I think it looks OK. I will blend into the background enough not to be especially noticed.

Mum looks up as I come into the kitchen. She has dark rings shadowing her eyes. I'm guessing she had another rough night with Amy.

"No uniform?" she says, sounding surprised.

"Yeah." I tug on my top. "It's for charity. I need to take in a pound."

Mum sighs. "A pound to wear your own stuff. . ." She reaches for her purse and digs around.

"Don't worry if you haven't got it," I say.

"I've got it," Mum mutters. She hands me the change. "Besides, some of my money comes in today. We should be OK."

"Are you sure?"

"I'm sure."

Her eyes settle on mine. I see that they soften slightly. She puts her purse down and walks towards me, gently grips my arms.

"You look lovely. Really grown up." She smiles. "Let me do your hair for you. I can put it in a nice high bun?"

I hesitate for a second, but then nod. "OK. . ."

She searches for the brush and then comes up behind me and begins to tug gently at hair. I usually hate for my hair to be messed around with. But weirdly today I kind of want it. I want to look different.

"I'm sorry about our argument the other day," she says as the brush sweeps through my hair. "I just hate all the questions, all the accusations. I want you to believe me this time. Ross isn't coming back."

I don't answer. My mouth is dry. I lick my lips.

"I know I made mistakes before, Alice, but this is different. I promise. I keep promising you this."

I flinch. The brush tugs at my skin. I turn my head a little. She is looking right at me, the brush is held mid-air, like she has paused, ready for me to say something. I almost go to tell her. I open my mouth ready to say something about the boy yesterday. I want to tell her how frightened

133

I am. How I can't work out if I'm being stupidly paranoid, or rightly scared.

But then she speaks again.

"I will keep us safe now, Alice." Her voice cracks. "I will not let you worry any more. I owe you that."

And just like that, my mouth closes again.

How can I say anything now?

The last dregs of students are trudging into the building when I arrive, so I join the queue. Everyone has made an effort. All I can see is flashes of designer labels and cool-looking trainers. It looks like a fashion parade here, not a school corridor. I hunch my shoulders forward and trail into my form room, trying to avoid eye contact.

It's loud in the room and of course Chloe and Esme are at the centre of the noise. Chloe is sitting on one of the tables, swinging her legs. She has the attention of most of the class. She is wearing skinny, dark jeans, boots and a black top that seems to hug all her curves. It's a simple outfit, but you can just tell it's expensive.

Esme is sitting next to her in a short skirt that shows off her long legs. She kicks out her feet purposely so that everyone can see her expensive trainers. They look brand new.

"Hey!" Chloe calls as I walk in. "Alice, you're late. We were just talking about you."

I sink into my seat quickly, eager to hide myself a little.

"Don't you want to know what we were saying?" Chloe asks sweetly.

"Not really." I make a big deal out of searching through my bag, looking like I've lost something.

"Nice hair," Esme says.

She and Chloe dissolve into giggles.

I glare back at her. What of it? I like my hair. Mum spent ages on it. So what, I don't look like every other kid here. Why do I have to?

"Thanks," I say, and smile.

"You certainly have your own look going on. . ." Chloe says, looking me up and down. "Is that top actually yours? It's a bit . . . old."

She says the word "old" like it's a bad word.

"It's just a top," I say.

But it really isn't and we both know that.

Esme sits back, crossing her arms a little. Her eyes widen. "Oh. . ." she says, all fake concern. "Oh, you poor thing. Did you not have anything else to wear?"

My skin is burning hot. I turn away from her. Words are dancing on my lips, words that I know if I let them escape will get me into a lot of trouble.

"If I'd thought about it, you could've worn something of mine," Chloe adds. "Well, something that I don't want any more."

"One of your cast-offs, you mean?" I snap. "No thanks. I'm good."

Both the girls stare at me, fighting smiles. "There's no need to get moody, Alice. We're only trying to help."

Yeah right.

"Do you not want to know what we were talking about earlier?" Chloe asks again, her voice smooth and sweet.

"No," I reply, not able to stand another word from her. "No, I couldn't care less."

"Fine. Be like that," she replies, sliding back into her chair. "But you'll wish you had."

I don't go to the hall at lunch. I'm not sure I can even face Ben today. I know he will be nice to me, but I don't need anyone's pity. Instead I sit in the toilets till lunch is over.

The worst thing is that Chloe and Esme are right. I do look a mess. I tug my hair free from my constricting bun and shake it free. I feel better already. But despite this I know the rest of me is all wrong. On the way back to class I see the flashes of colour that other people are wearing – well-fitting and expensive clothes – and I cringe inside. This stuff has never been important to me before, but today it's just another thing that marks me out as different. Another reason why I can't fit in with the rest.

And I hate it.

I try and get through the afternoon lessons the only way I know how, with my head down and my ears shut to everyone around me. That way I can almost pretend that I'm somewhere else – at the beach, or walking in the woods – anywhere but here. In English, my concentration slips totally and Mr Walker ends up shouting at me to "snap out of it". The rest of the class snigger and it's all I can do to sit still, my cheeks burning, muttering apologies that I don't mean.

When the last bell goes, I hurry off. I take the side exit, figuring that will be quieter – but I've totally misjudged it. As I turn the corner, down the snaky path that leads around the side of the school, I see a huddle of people standing in my way. Then I hear Chloe's distinctive high-pitched voice, projecting over everyone else.

"Hey! Alice – I wanted to talk to you."

I look up and force a half-smile like she doesn't bother me. Alfie says I can be scary when I want to be. When I first met him he used to think I was cocky and confident, but he couldn't be more wrong. That's just an act I put on to protect myself – like a cloak. Most of the time it works. But not always.

Chloe strolls over to me, away from the group.

"You were moody to me earlier," she says

coolly. "I was trying to be nice and you parred me."

"I didn't," I reply calmly.

Chloe smiles, but it doesn't reach her eyes. "I don't think you like me very much, Alice."

I snort. That makes two of us.

The rest of the group are watching us carefully. I recognize most of them as being popular girls from my year. They look at me as if I smell bad.

"It's not funny," Chloe tells me.

I stare at her and shrug. "I don't know what you want me to say."

"A sorry would be nice."

"Dream on."

She is smiling again. I've never realized before how ugly a smile can be. She reaches out and touches my top.

"Bless. . ." she says sweetly. "You couldn't even get today right, could you? Your clothes are as poor as you are."

The group snigger. I step back; I feel my hands clenching into fists.

"Don't touch me."

"Oh... Don't you like that?" Her long pointy finger pokes me again. "I'm only trying to help, Alice. You need a friend to tell you when you're looking a complete state."

"You're not my friend."

She looks up at me. Her eyes gleam. "No – I guess I'm not. Why would I want to be?" She giggles. "I guess I just felt sorry for you."

She feels sorry for me.

The blood races to my head. I can feel it pumping in my ears. Something is going to explode.

She feels sorry for me...

My mind is racing. I don't even think before I raise my fist.

Chapter Twelve

"I feel sorry for you. . ." Ross was looking at Mum, and his expression was one of disgust and pity. "That's all. I feel sorry for you."

But Mum just looked at him. She gave a quiet, disbelieving little laugh.

"You feel sorry for me?" she said, and she sounded so sad. So defeated.

And that was the worst thing – to hear her sounding so beaten.

You feel sorry for me. . .

The words that changed everything.

She repeated those words. She said them back

to him. Her voice was different now. Loud and angry. And then she laughed again. But this time the sound was so very different.

I can't remember that day, I won't—

My arm is going up when someone lays a hand on it. Ben.

"What's going on?" he asks.

"What's going on?" Chloe nearly screams. "This freak was going to hit me, that's what!"

I turn and see Ben staring at me, wide-eyed. "I came looking for you when you didn't meet me for lunch. . .." He frowns in Chloe's direction. "Seriously? You were going to hit her?"

Chloe rallies her group. "Isn't that right? She was going to hit me for absolutely no reason."

The brainless gaggle murmured their agreement.

"She was out of order," I whisper.

"I was just trying to be nice," Chloe throws back. "And this is all I get in return. No wonder you have no friends."

Ben squeezes my arm. "That's not true. She has me."

For some reason I blush hard. I turn my face away.

Chloe stares at the three of us for a few seconds, her mouth set in a firm line. She didn't count on this – on some boy from the year above coming to my defence.

"This doesn't look like very friendly behaviour to me," says Ben in that slow, lazy way of his. "This looks like mean girls baying for blood."

Chloe laughs. "What do you know about mean girls?"

Ben smiles, but his eyes are on Chloe. "Having an older sister helps; she's been through this stuff loads." His eyes narrow. "I know how nasty girls can be."

Chloe glares at us. "I don't know what you mean. I was just trying to help, Alice."

"How exactly?" I ask.

Her mouth opens and then closes again. Then she shrugs slowly.

"Well" – she reaches into her pocket – "I was going to give you this."

"What?" I'm thrown. This isn't what I was expecting.

Chloe reaches into her pocket and brings out a small, folded note. "I told you this morning that I had something to tell you."

"Just get on with it," Ben says, sounding bored.

Chloe hands me the note, offering me a sad smile at the same time. "Your stalker came to the school gate again this morning. He asked me to give you this. You really do know some strange people," Chloe shot at me before walking away. "I mean, who delivers notes? Hasn't he heard of a phone or whatever?"

We walk towards the beach and sit looking out to sea. It's a place me and Alfie have been so many times, and it seems so weird having Ben here too. The sea is wild today and the waves are crashing violently on the shore. I can feel the salty spray from here, cooling my hot face.

"I didn't know those girls were bothering you," Ben says at last. "You should have told me or Alfie."

"I don't need looking after," I mutter.

"I know you don't. But you do need friends," he replies firmly. "Everyone does."

"I'm doing just fine. I can deal with Chloe and her mates."

"Yeah! It looked like it. You were about to smash her face in."

"Not exactly. . ."

But wiping that smug grin off her face would've been nice.

"I could walk you back from school," Ben says. "I mean – if you want?"

I hesitate. But I don't want people feeling sorry for me. I don't need anyone's pity.

"I'm OK," I say finally. "But thank you."

"Well – the offer's there," he says.

I turn my attention back to the sea, back to the roaring waves. When we first moved here, I walked here and stood in a similar spot. It was the first thing I loved about this place – the force and beauty of that water. It was the first time I'd ever been so close to it. I'd only lived in London before. The sea was a faraway place that I read about in books or saw in films and TV shows – and yet here it was.

So close. I was literally standing at the edge of the country, looking out at something else, something I couldn't see – other places, other possibilities.

"So . . . what does it say?"

My gaze drifts down to my hand and to the note still pressed between my fingers. Something is stopping me opening it.

"You need to read it," Ben says softly. "You need to find out why he's been following you. If he's anything to do with Ross."

He's right of course.

"It doesn't make sense," I say. "I saw him yesterday. I chased after him but he ran away. If he wanted to talk – why didn't he stop then?"

Ben shrugs. I open the note. It's a small piece of paper, like a page torn from an exercise book. The writing on it is scrawled, but neat.

Alice

I'm sorry if we freaked you out. My brother, Tommy, came home yesterday and told me what happened. He wasn't meant to run away like that. He was just meant to find

out where you live and tell me. I work a lot,
you see, so it's harder for me to do.

Anyway. I'm making a mess of this. I was
hoping you'd be on Facebook or something,
but you're not anywhere.

Alice – the thing is, I think we're related.

I need to explain a few things. Please call me
or text me. I'll come and meet you. We can talk.

Love
Jas (Jasmine) x

Underneath is a scrawled number.

"Jas." I say the name out loud. It sounds so strange. So alien.

"Who is she?" Ben asks, and then frowns a little. "I mean, I'm guessing it is a girl?"

"Yes. Jas – Jasmine."

I squint at the words again. It's as if nothing is sinking in. I can't seem to take in this information. I look up and I'm light-headed.

"Are you OK?" he asks, lightly touching my arm.

"Yes – I. . . She says she thinks we're related. I've never heard of a Jas before, not from Mum. . ."

"Do you think she's for real?"

I shake my head softly, uncertain. Could this be a trap? Ross's sick way of making me get in contact again?

Ben looks thoughtfully at the note. "Alice, do you think this could be—" He pauses, shakes his head. "Oh, I dunno. It's probably silly of me to say to it."

"What?"

"I just wondered if this Jas could be linked to your dad. Your real dad?"

The letter in my hand suddenly feels hot. I almost drop it. My real dad? Why hadn't I considered that?

"I don't think. . ." My thoughts drift, tumbling clumsily together. "My mum says she doesn't even know where he is. How would he, or anyone linked to him, know where I was?"

"Anyone can be found nowadays," Ben says. "In the end."

I can't answer that. I don't know what to say.

"What are you going to do?" he asks.

"I'm going to call her. I'll meet her," I say, suddenly sure. "I need to know who she is."

I need answers.

Chapter Thirteen

The house is strangely quiet when I walk in. No one is here. The living room is still a mess. Amy's toys are everywhere. Her play mat is spread out in the centre of the room. On the small coffee table, I can see Henry has been colouring. His crayons are spilled out, leaving smudges of colour on the surface. I quickly gather them up and stuff them back into the packet. I imagine the mess if they were trod into the carpet.

Ross would go mad.

I stop myself. Seriously! I'm doing it again. He's back in my head. Taunting me.

Go away! I don't want you back!

I walk through to the kitchen. It's cleaner in here. It always is. I instinctively flinch as a memory takes hold.

Ross was gripping Mum's hand and walking her over to the sink, really slow. His entire body was stiff, like a rod about to strike. Mum's body was limp, like a rag doll. She'd given up. She knew what was coming.

I stood back. I could feel the prickles of tension from the other side of the room.

His other hand pressed the small of her back. He made her bend forward, forced her to. Her face was almost jammed up against the tap.

"Just look at that. . . Look. . ."

"I'm sorry." Mum's words. They were automatic now. She said them so much. It never did any good.

"You know I hate mess."

"It's just potato peelings. . . I'll. . ."

He pressed her forward more. I could see the grip on her wrist was tightening. "Are we animals?"

His voice so smooth and gentle. So silky.

"I'm sorry, Ross, but you wanted mash tonight. I was going to sort this out."

"So this is my fault?"

His voice changed. Deeper now. More a growl. I knew what was coming. The chill drenched my skin.

I walked out of the room. I didn't want to see what was going to happen next.

My mind whirred. I sucked in a breath as I slipped up the stairs. I closed the door of my room. I closed my eyes and my ears.

It was her fault. She should've kept it clean. She should've known.

It was her fault.

And now. Even now, our kitchen is sparkling. Every surface. Every drawer front. The smell of bleach always makes me want to choke. Is it any wonder I hate being in here? It's as if he is still standing at the door, inspecting the room with that hateful stare of his. I leave the room quickly and call upstairs instead. Where is she?

As if on cue, my phone buzzes.

I pull it out. Mum.

The text is brief.

Just popped out to meet a friend. Henry's
on a play date. Back about six-ish.

There's pasta in the fridge if you're
hungry.

I stare at the words. Friend? Mum doesn't have
any friends any more.

It's only then that my eyes fall on the little pad
by the sink. It's the one my mum always makes
her notes in. Today there's only one thing written
down. A giant capital *R*, ringed around several
times and underneath *6 p.m.* scrawled down.

R.

Ross.

Surely?

Mum is lying to me again.

I run upstairs. Of course it's Ross. It's who I've
suspected all along. It explains all the secret texts
and the strange behaviour. Mum can't keep away
from him.

I wonder what he's promised her this time. An
amazing holiday? A new car? Never to smack her
head again for not getting dinner ready on time?

He's good at making promises – but not so good at keeping them.

Tears are building up in my eyes. I was thinking of showing Mum the letter from Jas, asking if she knew anything. But now I can't trust her. I have to do this on my own. I head for her room. I know that she has a box full of stuff, mainly keepsakes, where she kept the picture of Dad before she gave it to me. I've only seen the box a handful of times and I've never been allowed to look through it, it's always been hidden out of sight. I hesitate in the doorway of her room. Mum and I respect each other's privacy and space and would never think to invade it or spy on each other; it's like an unwritten rule between us. I've never even come close to breaking it before. She's never come in my room without knocking either.

And yet here I am now, walking into her room. It's tidy in here too. There's really not much furniture, just the bed from the council and the ancient wardrobe and chest of drawers that were here before we moved in. So apart from Amy's cot and a couple of still unpacked boxes, there's not much else in here. I take a deep breath and head towards her wardrobe.

I am crossing a line.

I go to her wardrobe first because it seems like the most logical place to start, but inside there is nothing apart from a small selection of her clothes hanging up. Mum doesn't have many clothes now. A lot of them she left behind the last time we left Ross – including all the expensive dresses he bought her. Looking at the rather drab and small collection that she has now makes my stomach ache.

Why am I doing this?

I slam the doors shut again.

I go to the chest of drawers next. I tug open each drawer and run my hand through the neatly folded clothes. The top drawer has a small selection of Mum's things – the lower two are full of Henry's and Amy's. *We have so little*, I think, remembering the racks of expensive clothes, the toys, the books we used to have.

I walk over to her bed. It's neatly made, and

I can see the T-shirt that Mum sleeps in, folded under the pillow. Lying on top of it is Henry's dressing gown and one of Amy's dummies. I move closer and notice something else.

There, tucked under the second pillow, is another T-shirt. I pull it out, but even without seeing it I know whose it is.

Ross.

It was one of his favourites. A soft faded grey one with a picture of old-school Space Invaders on it. He used to wear it around the house and joke about the days when "gaming was good". I bring the top to my face. I can still smell him. That sharp, almost fruity scent of the aftershave he used to wear. Bile rises in my throat.

I hear the front door slam and my entire body freezes. I shove the T-shirt back under the pillow and then I quickly and quietly move out of her bedroom – praying that a dodgy floorboard doesn't give me away.

"Alice!" she calls.

"I'm just up here!" I shout back. I dart into the toilet and out again, shaking my hands as though I've just washed them. Mum is coming up the stairs when I step back out on to the landing.

"Are you OK? Your face is all red," she asks.

"I'm fine."

"Are you sure?" She frowns. "Did you have a bad day at school?"

School? That seems so long ago now that I have to pause and think.

"It wasn't great," I say finally. "Some girls were being a bit mean."

"Oh, love. What happened?" She steps towards me, touches my cheek. It's all I can do not to flinch. "Do you need me to talk to school?"

"No. It's sorted now. Ben helped."

"Oh." Mum smiles. "Isn't he Alfie's friend?"

"Yes."

"That's nice then? That he helped you out today. He must be a good lad too?"

"I guess. . ." I glance back up at her. She looks different. I can see she's wearing make-up and her hair is all shiny and freshly brushed. She's glowing. She looks happy, but nervous too.

"Who was this friend you went to see?" I ask finally.

"Oh, just someone..." Her cheeks redden. "An old friend, before your time. It was nice to catch up." I stare at her and she flushes deeper. "I'll tell you all about it soon. But trust me, Alice. It's all good."

Chapter Fourteen

I don't want to keep remembering it, but of course I do. It's like my brain is a TV stuck on a loop and it keeps playing the same scene over and over.

I'm forced to relive it. Especially now, late at night when there are no other distractions. No one else to talk to.

She had said, in that hard voice: "You feel sorry for me?"

And then she had laughed. Not a normal sort of laugh. This one was loud and hollow. This was an "I don't care any more" sort of sound.

It was chilling.

I was seated on the chair opposite them. Ross was on the sofa next to Mum. I saw his entire body stiffen at the sound of her laughter. His face became a fixed mask again. The snarl was painted across it, he didn't even bother to hide it this time. The monsters were real and he was sitting here with us.

"Mum—"

I tried to stop her. I knew that this was going to be bad. I knew I had to stop her.

But she just kept laughing. She kept on and on.

Ross thumped the armrest and swore loudly.

"Stop that now!"

She didn't.

"You feel sorry for me." She gasped. "How funny is that? How bloody funny. . ."

I didn't see what was so funny and neither did Ross. He jumped up. His large body loomed over hers. He was twice her size. He swallowed her up.

I called out for him to stop. He couldn't hear

me. Neither of them could hear me. It was like I didn't exist. I shouted again for them to listen.

But they didn't.

So I did the only thing I could to make it stop.

I wake up late because of my bad night and have to rush. I barely have time to kiss Henry and Amy before flying out of the front door.

"You need to eat something," Mum shouts after me.

"I'll grab something on the way," I lie.

It's a relief not to have to sit and eat with her. I need some time to get my head around everything and decide what I want to say first. But one thing is for sure: if Mum is taking Ross back, this time I'm not sticking around.

I walk to school, my heart racing. I feel sick and my head is fuzzy from lack of sleep. My eyes feel raw.

"Hey!"

I look up. Waiting at the end of the main road is Alfie.

"I thought you had football practice?" I say.

He shrugs. "Didn't fancy it today."

"So you thought you'd walk all the way up here?"

He shrugs. "To be honest I needed the walk. I wanted some space, you know."

"Oh. . . OK. . ." I nod. That usually means he's having sad thoughts about his mum. I've learnt it's best not to press him on this. If he wants to talk to me he will.

We walk on in silence for a bit and then Alfie speaks again.

"Ben told me about the note and what happened yesterday."

"I thought he would," I say. "It's all so crazy."

"Did you ring it? The number?"

"No. . ."

"Why not?"

"I dunno – I just. . ." I shake my head, feeling silly. "It just feels like a big deal. What if I mess it up? What if I say the wrong thing?"

He stops walking and turns to face me. "Alice. I just know you won't. This is you. You are good at dealing with things like this."

"Really? You think so?"

He shrugs again. "Sure. You're about the most 'together' person I know." He pauses. "But to be fair, my best mate is Ben, so. . ."

I laugh. "Where even is he today?"

I don't say it out loud, but I kind of miss him. Obviously I love having Alfie with me, he's my mate. But there's something about Ben's lazy smile that makes me instantly relax.

"Probably slept in. Did you show your mum the note?"

I shake my head. "Alfie, I can't. I'm pretty sure she's seeing Ross again. . . My head is a mess. I need some answers."

"So call that number then." Alfie nudges me gently. "It might help. You need some of these questions answered or you'll drive yourself mad."

We stop. I pull out my phone. I'd already saved Jas's number in there for when I was ready. Slowly I open up the tab and scroll down to her name. My thumb hovers above it.

"Really?" I say.

"Yes! Do it."

I press down before I can stop myself and hold the phone hard against my ear. As the number rings I feel my stomach flip over. I'm actually glad I didn't eat anything this morning.

The number keeps ringing and then flicks over to voicemail. "Hi. This is Jas. Leave me a message and I'll get back to you."

Her voice is light. Friendly. Young.

Then the bleep. I flinch. What the hell do I say?

"Hi, Jas. This is Alice. You left a note for me. I'm calling you back like you asked – I'd really like to know who you are and how you think you know me. Thank you."

I hang up and stare and Alfie. I feel breathless.

He nods. "That was cool. Now hopefully she'll call back."

"Hopefully," I reply.

What if Jas is bad news? I think. Someone I shouldn't be in contact with. What if I've just opened a whole can of worms?

I put my phone away and we start walking again.

"You should feel a bit better now," Alfie says

softly. "You're doing something proactive. You're helping yourself."

"What about you?" I ask. "How can we help you feel better?"

It just slips out, I don't mean it to.

"Why do you ask that?"

"I dunno." I shrug. "I just know you're still hurting about your mum. I wish there was more I could do."

He stops. His face has gone all hard. "And you think I should just *feel better*? I lost my mum."

"Alfie. . ." I start.

I want to tell him that it's OK. He doesn't need to "feel better". I shouldn't have said that. It was stupid of me. But he interrupts me before I get the chance.

"It was her birthday yesterday," he says flatly.

"Oh, Alfie. . ."

"That's why I wasn't around yesterday. I didn't have football practice. I wanted to be at home, with Dad."

"I get that," I say.

He shakes his head slowly. "Just like that,

it's here and she's not, so I'm not sure it even counts."

"Of course it counts. It'll always count."

His head seems to sink further into his body. "I think I'm getting over it, Alice, but it's so hard. . ."

"I know. I know it is." I touch his arm. "But you're not alone, OK. You know that. You've got me. And Ben."

He nods.

"You've always got me."

He wipes his arm across his face. "OK."

We walk the rest of the way in silence, but it's a peaceful sort of silence. At the school gate Alfie turns to me and half smiles.

"Thank you. I knew it would help seeing you."

And something about those words makes me glow from the inside.

I helped him. I did some good.

Me.

I shuffle through the day. That's the only way to describe it really. I guess I'm hoping that if I keep my head down and try and ignore the rest of the world, they might forget I'm there.

Weirdly, today it seems to work. Esme and Chloe keep their distance. They stare at me like I'm some kind of weird species of animal, but they don't say anything nasty. Esme even flashes me a wary smile, which is a bit unsettling, and Chloe just looks uncomfortable.

Anyway. I've got more important things to think about.

I check my phone at lunch – nothing from Jas. Alfie and Ben try to cheer me up as I chew on my dry sandwich, but it's no good.

"She's probably changed her mind," I say. "Or maybe it was some kind of joke."

"Have faith," Alfie says. "It's still early. She said she worked a lot."

"I guess."

Last class is English, so not the worst. The final bell is such a relief I almost cry out. Once again I pull out my phone, but yet again there's nothing there.

I think of the walk home, of facing Mum. Of

the secrets she's keeping from me. I wish there was somewhere else, anywhere else, that I could go.

Then I remember that there is.

As soon as I walk into the art room, I see him. Ben. He's sitting right at the back, where I usually sit. For a moment I'm frozen. It seems weird seeing him out of context. I'm used to seeing him in the canteen, slouched over his milkshake, or strolling along with Alfie laughing loudly. Yet here he's quiet, serious, bent over a piece of work. He looks startled to see me and then recovers, and gives me a small wave.

Ms Monroe comes over to me, smiling widely.

"Alice. You came! I'm so pleased. You can see it's just a small group at the moment, but I'm hoping we can help to inspire each other."

There are a few others here. A small group of year eleven girls who I don't know. Two boys, who look older. Another boy from my year – Reece? And Lauren, sitting at the front again. She looks up and smiles at me.

"We are working on emotions at the moment," Ms Monroe says. "Trying to draw how we feel on paper."

"OK…" I nod and sit myself down near Lauren. Ben is absorbed in his work again.

"This is really hard," Lauren whispers at me.

I look over at her paper. She's drawing flowers, but they are drooping and dying. I immediately feel a wave of sadness.

"That's really good," I tell her.

"Is it?" She stares at the page. "I think it might be a bit – well, obvious – but it kind of represents my mood."

"I don't even know where to start," I say.

"Just use your instinct. What comes straight into your mind."

I almost laugh at that. My mind is so jumbled, so full up. And of course that's when my pencil starts to move. I sketch out shapes, lines – chaos.

My cluttered thoughts.

"It's very abstract," Lauren says after a bit. "But it's really effective."

"Thank you." I smile. "I actually quite like it."

And weirdly I feel lighter somehow, like I've managed to spill some of the clutter out on to the page.

"Well done for standing up to Chloe and Esme," Lauren goes on. "Those two are complete cows."

I pause. "What did you hear?"

Lauren grins at me. "The rumour is that you were going to punch both of them, but your boyfriend stopped you."

"Boyfriend?" My cheeks are already starting to blaze. "I haven't got a boyfriend."

"Oh – isn't that him over there?" Lauren waves a pencil in Ben's direction. "I see you together a lot."

"No way," I say quickly. "He's just a friend."

"Oh. . . Shame. He's cute." She grins.

I look over towards Ben just as he glances in my direction. He smiles his lazy smile and my stomach flips over.

"He makes you go red too." Lauren nudges me.

"It's nothing. . ." I stammer. "Honestly . . . he's my mate's best mate."

"Well, like I said. Shame." Lauren sets down

her pencil and yawns. She's really pretty, with wide eyes and thick lashes. "We should hang out sometime?"

"Really?"

"Oh god, yeah. Seriously. You're like my hero right now for standing up to the gruesome twosome." She drops her voice a little. "Although you could have gone the extra mile and punched both of them."

We both dissolve in giggles.

"That's enough for today," Ms Monroe calls out.

Ben comes over to me as I'm packing up my things. Lauren raises her eyebrow at me and then slips out.

"I didn't realize you were coming," he says, grinning slightly. "That was a nice surprise."

"Really?" I smile back, not sure what to say.

"Wow, I love your piece. It's very – I dunno – Kandinsky-like."

"Do you think?" I squint at it. "It looks a bit messy, doesn't it? But it certainly reflects my mood. What did you do?"

He reaches across the table and slides his

paper towards me. For a moment I can't say anything. Ben has drawn his face, but it has been beautifully, precisely fractured into tiny sections. It's so detailed, it's breathtaking.

"You feel . . . broken?" I ask tentatively.

"No! Not broken. Just incomplete, I think. Like there's bits missing." He ruffles his hair. "I guess that sounds weird, right?"

"No. Not at all." I pause. "This is so good. I mean, you are really good."

He ducks his head a little. "Thank you."

I pick up my bag and we both wave goodbye to Ms Monroe, who is in deep conversation with one of the year elevens. As we move through the door, Ben touches my arm. I swear a tiny electrical pulse trickles through my skin.

"Can I walk back with you?" he asks.

"Isn't it out of your way?"

"Maybe." He is smiling, but it's a shy smile this time. "I need the exercise."

We walk out of the building together and it's odd, like something has shifted between us, and I'm not sure what to make of it.

"I like being with you," he says softly.
"I like being with you too. . ." I reply.
And just then, my phone rings.

Chapter Fifteen

"Alice?" Ben nudges me. "Quickly. It'll ring off soon."

I quickly hunt around in my bag and pull my mobile out. I look down at the number calling me. It's her. It's Jas.

I glance up at Ben.

"It'll be OK," he says. His eyes are on mine. "Just answer it."

I swipe the screen.

"Hello. . ." I croak. I cough and try again. "Hi. Is that Jas?"

"Yes – yes, it is. Is that Alice?" The voice is confident, warm. "Oh my god. Is it Alice?"

"Yes . . . yes, it is."

A pause. "I can't believe I've actually found you." She is talking quickly now, like she can barely contain her excitement. "Do you know how long it's taken to find you?"

"Who are you?" I say.

She pauses. "So he didn't tell you either."

"I don't know who you're talking about," I say uncertainly.

"Your dad," she says. "Or should I say *our* dad."

"Our dad?" I repeat this back. It sounds so wrong on my tongue. I've never called anyone that before, not even Ross. "Hey, wait a minute, are you saying you're . . . my sister?"

She laughs. "That's what I'm saying. So, you really didn't know about me?"

I take a deep breath. "No – I didn't. I've never even seen my Dad. He left before I was born."

Jas swears under her breath. "Oh man, I'm sorry this must be full on. I'll explain, shall I?"

I give a shaky laugh. "That would be nice."

"He left us when I was nearly five. All my mum knew was that Dad had got another young girl pregnant while he was still with her. He left us not long after. My mum and yours had a shared friend, so she got the odd detail about you. For ages I wasn't fussed. Mum said we were better off without him, without any connection to him. Then I grew older and started asking questions. I wanted to meet my little sister. But by the time I started looking for you, you had moved away. My mum tried writing to the new address we had in London but no answer. You wanted a fresh start, I guess?"

"Yeah," I mutter.

A fresh start. Yeah, that was right. Mum had moved away from here to our first little flat. And then she had met Ross. No one would've found us there.

"But I kept asking people if they'd seen you. I never gave up. And then one day recently that same friend, this woman called Lorraine, she said your mum was back in contact with her and that you'd moved back here. She gave me this address."

I rub my forehead. "If your mum wrote, why did Mum never tell me?"

"I don't know. Maybe she never got the letters. Maybe she didn't want to know."

"So you tracked me down," I say softly. "You sent someone to follow me to school. To watch me at football games. . ."

"My little brother wanted to help, said he'd stop you after school. But he's so shy it's not even funny. He did a runner when you tried to talk to him. I'm sorry if he freaked you out." She paused. "I was going to come myself, but I've been working crazy long hours. I also wanted to check you were legit too. We've had a few false starts."

There's a long silence. Ben is watching me, but I can't think of anything to say. I feel uneasy. I don't know what to believe, who to trust.

Jas coughs softly. "Alice – I would love to meet you." I don't say anything. "I'm your sister. Well – your half-sister. I'm family. I want to get to know you. When I found you, I was so excited. I understand this might be too much for you, but I'm hoping. . ."

Another silence. And then I whisper, "I want to get to know you too."

Because I do. Of course I do.

She gives a little shriek of excitement and I laugh.

"So we can do this?" she says. "We can meet up?"

"Yes," I say.

"Can you do tomorrow? Is that too soon?" she asks.

I need to meet her somewhere safe. Someplace I know well.

"Come to the beach," I say. "There's a tree there. Opposite the promenade. You can't miss it. It's all burnt up and ruined. We can meet by there."

"OK. Cool. Is four OK? And listen, you should tell your mum. If you want to. Because I want to meet her, too."

"Four is perfect. I'll make a call on Mum." I pause. The uneasy feeling still won't go. "Jas, your brother – you said he came to the school and the football. But he came to my house too, right? I saw him."

There's a silence. Then Jas says slowly, "He

came once, but only to see if we had your address right. We weren't getting a reply, so I wanted to check. He wasn't sure when he went to the house, so that's when we thought we'd try the school."

"But he only came that time?" I insist.

"Yeah – just one time. I swear. We never wanted to freak you out or anything."

"And he didn't post anything?"

"No. Of course not."

"OK," I say. I feel numb. Talking to Jas has explained so much, but not everything. I saw someone outside my house twice, not once. And someone delivered a letter through the door. It still doesn't add up.

"I'll see you tomorrow," she says softly.

"Yeah, tomorrow," I reply.

I hang up.

"So you're going to meet?" Ben asks.

"Yeah, but. . ." I shake my head, swallowing hard. "She says her brother came to my house." I pause. "But he only came the once. So someone else was standing outside my place. Someone else posted a letter. I know they did."

I stop. Ben has gone bright red.

"What?" I ask. "Ben. What is it?"

"I'm so sorry, Alice," he says. "That person outside your house the other time . . . it was me."

I stare at him for a moment. I shake my head a little to clear it. "What? I don't understand."

Ben can't even look at me, he's staring at the ground. His hair has fallen in front of his face so that I can't read his expression.

"Ben?" I say, more firmly. "What were you doing there?"

"Being an idiot." Finally he looks up. He slowly brushes his hair away from his eyes. His cheeks are bright red. "I came to see you. I wanted to knock at your door – to talk to you – but I couldn't do it. . . I chickened out."

None of this makes any sense. This was Ben. Loud, confident Ben. I don't recognize this person.

"I came to your house to see you, but when I got there I just bottled it. I hung around for a bit because I thought I might bump into you outside. I thought maybe that would be easier. That's all, I swear."

"That's all! You scared me," I snap back.

"I'm sorry. . ." he says weakly. "I was so lame."

I take a deep breath. "So, you came to talk to me, but instead you just stood outside, like a creepy stalker?"

"But that's why I wrote the letter!"

A letter. I stare at him open-mouthed. The letter that Henry had seen. The one that Mum must've thrown away.

"I was convinced Ross had contacted Mum again. I thought she was lying to me. And it was just you acting like a primary school kid and posting me a childish note!"

He flinches. "I'm sorry, Alice," he says. "I didn't think about the whole Ross thing. I never thought you'd make that connection with him."

"Yeah. You didn't think, that's the problem."

I slip my phone into my bag and ease it back over my shoulder. Then I turn and start to walk.

"Wait," he says, jogging after me. "Just wait a minute."

"I need to get home," I say tightly. "It's getting late.

"Alice, come on," he pleads. "I was stupid. But

now that you know the truth – that it was just me, that it was no big deal—"

I freeze. It's like he has pressed an old bruise on my skin. The pain bleeds into me.

I spin around and I know my eyes are blazing. I can feel the rage burning through me.

"No big deal?" I interrupt, my voice as cold as ice. "Do you know how many days I've spent worrying that my mum's ex-boyfriend had come back and found us? Do you even know what's like?" I shake my head at him slowly. "No, of course you don't. Why would you? You've never had to move from house to house, waiting for him to find you. You've never had to lie in bed at night wondering whether he'll come to the door. You've always been safe."

He ducks his head a little. "I'm sorry. I should've realized."

"You knew I was scared," I said. "I told you. And you could have explained. You could've made it better."

"I've told you now," he says. "Alice, I didn't mean to hurt you."

"It's too late now," I reply, my voice cracking.

I didn't mean to hurt you.

I walk away quickly.

He doesn't follow and I'm glad.

Chapter Sixteen

People should take notice of me. People should listen!

I'm back there again. The memory is as raw and fresh as if it had just happened.

Ross is screaming at Mum. Mum is laughing and crying at the same time and I'm shouting. I'm shouting at then to see me.

I launched myself between them. Ross let go of Mum. She cried out and fell back on to the sofa and Ross's free-falling arm came down crashing towards me.

Time slowed. It must have, because I had time

to look up at his face, to see him clearly. His eyes were wet, his jaw was locked in a cruel grimace, spit was bubbling at the corner of his lips.

How did we ever think he was handsome? Some kind of prince?

He was ugly, ugly, ugly.

I should have jumped aside. I should've moved. But I didn't. I was frozen.

I didn't see his hand rising. I heard a slapping sound. Light danced in front of my eyes. Someone was shouting. I think it was my mum, but I wasn't sure.

Maybe it was me?

I reached up and touched my nose.

My fingers curled in front of my face. I could see blood. I couldn't feel any pain at all and yet there was all this sticky red stuff on my hands.

I looked back up at Ross.

His fist was still raised, but the rage has gone. I could see that now. His eyebrows are furrowed. His mouth tightened.

And then I realized that he was crying.

My mum began to howl.

I raised my hand to my nose, drew it away and stared at my hand. I could hardly believe what I was seeing. Who knew blood was so red? I don't think I was scared at all. I was just puzzled. Surprised maybe.

No one had ever hit me before. Ross was still crying. He came towards me, his arms outstretched, but I backed away. I didn't want him to touch me. I think it was then when I realized my whole body was shaking.

Mum came up behind me. Her arms wrapped around me. She felt so incredibly strong. She whispered into my ear.

"I'm sorry, Alice. Oh god. I'm so sorry."

Everything else happened quickly. We were moving. Mum dragged me upstairs, while I still clutched my bloody nose. It was really hurting by now. I wanted to curl up in bed. I didn't want to do anything else – but Mum suddenly had this energy. Ross followed, pleading, sobbing, shouting. She didn't speak to him, not once. Just shut the bedroom door in his face.

She rang for a taxi, all the while grabbing

clothes out of drawers, stuffing them into a rucksack. Like before, but different somehow. As she scooped Amy out of her cot and gently coaxed Henry awake I saw something in her eyes that hadn't been there before. A hardness.

"Where are we going. . .?" Henry moaned.

"We're going somewhere safe," she said.

I started crying then. I didn't want to leave, to go to another hostel, another B & B.

"Please don't make us leave," I said. "It was my fault."

Mum froze. Then, slowly, she reached towards my face. Her hand lightly stroked my hair. Her eyes met mine.

"Don't ever say that again," she said. "Don't ever say it was your fault. This was him. It was always him." She shivered and let her hand fall. "I'll never let him hurt any of us again."

She picked up the few bags we had, hitched Amy on her hip and told me to take Henry's hand. As we hurried down the stairs, I expected to see Ross, trying to block the way. Usually he followed us out, laughing and shouting that we'd be back. But he was just standing to one side. He looked like a much smaller, shrunken version of himself.

"You don't need to do this," he said.

"Yes. Yes, I do," Mum said.

He looked at me. He looked embarrassed. Like Henry when he'd been caught doing something he shouldn't.

"I'm sorry, Alice," he said. "I didn't mean to hurt you. I didn't see you."

Those ended up being the last words he said to me as we slammed out into the cold night.

I walk fast away from Ben, the wind stinging my eyes. I thought we were free then, really free. And yet here I am again and Mum is texting Ross, and some other guy is muttering the same words to me. "I didn't mean to hurt you."

He didn't see me either. He didn't see the fear I was in. The pain he put me through.

Why didn't he see?

Henry is bouncing off the walls when I get home, so, partly to avoid seeing Mum, I take him out in the garden and try half-heartedly to play football with him.

"I want Alfie," Henry complains when I miss yet another ball. "When is he coming round again?"

"I don't know."

I don't want to think about Alfie. Ben is bound to tell him what has happened. He and Ben have been friends for ever. Will he even understand why I got so freaked out, or will he think I was just overreacting? Even the thought of losing Alfie as a mate is making me feel sick.

"I hope he comes soon," Henry says.

"So do I."

Finally, we go back inside. I hesitate by the sitting room, where I can see Mum on the couch. Henry scoots past me, keen to watch some TV before bedtime.

Mum is curled up, reading a magazine. She looks relaxed and happy.

"Hello, love," she says. "Give me five minutes and I'll get some tea on."

I take another step into the room. As if on

cue, her phone buzzes with a message, and she reads it.

"Who's that?" I say.

Mum glances up. "Oh – nothing."

"You keep saying that," I say. "You keep telling me it's nothing. But it has to be someone."

She pushes her hair away from her face and looks at me closely. "What are you worried about, Alice?" she asks, gently.

"So it's not Ross?" The words burst out of me before I can stop them. Mum rocks back a little on her chair.

"Alice, no – why would you think that?"

"I don't know. . ." I shrug. "All of your secretive texting. The meetings. It seems familiar somehow."

Mum stands. Then she speaks very quietly and slowly. "I promised you, Alice. I will never get in contact with Ross again. You can trust me on this one, I swear."

Trust. Such a simple word, but it hangs between us like one of those bullets that you see in really old cartoons – suspended in air – waiting to blast through me.

Trust. I spent years trusting her, believing her when she said we would be safe, only for her to take us back to him.

Mum reaches for me, but I flinch away.

"Ross has gone," she says firmly. "I will keep telling you this until you believe me. Ross has gone and he will never ever come back. I will never let that happen."

"So who have you been meeting?" I hiss.

"It's no one you would know, love. A friend from long ago, from when I used to live here, as a teenager. We were in the same care home. I guess you could say she was the only friend I really had back then. We ran into each other recently and she gave me her number, so I got back in touch. Her name is Lorraine. *Lorraine.*"

Before I can stop myself I say, "Jas told me about her."

It's Mum's turn to look confused. "Jas? Who is Jas?"

I guess there's no point going back now.

"She's my half-sister, Mum. She's found me."

Mum swallows. "Jasmine. So you know."

I stare back at her, willing her to continue, and she does.

"Jasmine is Carmel's daughter. Carmel was with your dad before I met him." She pauses. "The thing you have to remember, Alice, is that I was so young when I met your dad. So very young and naive. I didn't really think about what else was going on. When he told me he had finished with this Carmel girl, I believed him. I'd believe anything he said."

"But he hadn't."

Mum snorted. "Of course he hadn't. I'm ashamed now, looking back. I mean, I knew he had a child with her, but he told me so much nonsense. Said the baby wasn't his. Rubbish like that. And the fool I was, I believed him, for a bit. He was sneaky like that. He would charm you and make you think he was the nicest person in the world, but in reality he could never speak a word of truth. The only person he cared for was himself. I guess growing up in care had made me a bit vulnerable. I was desperate for someone to love. For a brief time I thought your dad could love and look after me. But it was clear he couldn't."

"But in the end you left him?"

"Yeah … in the end." Mum sighs heavily and sits back down. "I told him about you, that I was pregnant of course, but he wasn't interested. By then I knew the truth about Carmel. I knew her little girl was his. He was still seeing her all the time he was with me." Her eyes meet mine. "I'm sorry, Alice. I wish I could say your dad was a nice person, but the truth is he wasn't. It was my friend Lorraine who told me the truth. She knew about Carmel and how she was struggling with her little three-year-old girl. How she loved him too. When she told me that, there was no going back. I would rather that he went back to her, tried to make it work for the sake of the child who already knew him. As it turns out, he couldn't even bring himself to do that…"

"So you didn't see him again."

"Not really, no. He came over a few times after you were born and gave us a bit of money, but that was it. The last I heard he had left town for a new job miles away. That was years ago."

I nod slowly, taking it all in. All these years of knowing nothing at all, and now it's all too much.

"Why didn't you tell me about her before? She's my half-sister, Mum. She's my family!"

Mum looks away. "Lorraine's been begging me to tell you. She's mates with Carmel too, says they're a nice family, that they know about you, kept saying you two girls should meet – but I kept putting it off." She spreads her hands in front of her. "I don't even know why. You'd been through so much. I wanted you to settle in a bit, before I told you."

"So you're not angry that I know?"

Mum sighs again. "No, not really. I'm relieved. The truth had to come out." Her eyes are sparkling with tears. "I was so happy to see Rainey. I realized how much I needed her and missed her. How much I wanted my best friend back in my life – someone I could love and trust. . ." She smiles softly. "You'd love her, Alice. You were so little when we moved away the first time, but Rainey always was so good with you."

"Rainey?"

Of course. The *R* on the pad. It all makes sense now.

"Rainey is the best friend I ever had. I wanted her back. Ross hated me staying in contact with my friends, he put an end to all that. But coming back here, I knew what I needed," Mum says. "And it was you who made me realize that, Alice."

"Me? How?"

"Because of your friendship with Alfie." Mum smiles sadly. "It reminded me of something that I once had and nearly destroyed."

"Oh." I don't know what to say.

"Go and meet with Jas, find out everything you can about her. If you want to, then do it," she says, her eyes locked on mine. "I'm just so sorry you've had to wait this long before finding out you had a sister."

"It's OK," I say finally.

"Really?"

"Really."

Because I understand why sometimes running away can seem easier than facing up to things.

But I'm done running.

Chapter Seventeen

It's nearly four p.m. Alfie calls me as I walk down towards the seafront. I'm surprised. He never usually rings me. He's more a texting kind of person.

"Hey," I say.

"Hey," he replies. "I thought I'd check in. You OK?"

I take a breath and then slowly start to explain the whole story to him. Jas. My mum keeping her a secret from me. My mum's friend Rainey and then finally Ben turning out to be the mystery watcher. I struggle with the last bit, worried about what he'll say, but he just groans softly.

"So, in short," I finish, "I have a sister I didn't know. I accused my mum of seeing Ross again when she isn't. And Ben, who I thought was actually kind of cool, is in fact a weirdo stalker."

Alfie lets out a long breath. "Wow, Alice – that's a lot to take in. What are you doing now?"

"I'm on my way to meet Jas." My stomach clenches. "Oh god, Alfie. I'm actually doing this. I'm going to meet her."

"You'll be fine," he says firmly. "She's your sister, not anything scary."

Sister – even the word sounds wrong. A few days ago I only knew of one sister, and cute as she is, it would be nice to have one who understands stuff a bit more.

"She might hate me," I say finally.

"She won't. No one can hate you, Alice."

"I wouldn't be so sure about that." I swallow. "I don't know if I can do this."

"How about I come too? It won't take me five minutes to run down."

My heart leaps. "Would you? But hang on – you have training, don't you?"

"I can miss one session. You need a mate. I'm coming. OK?"

"OK," I say.

"*And* it'll give me a chance to talk to you properly about Ben."

My stomach flips again. "Oh no, Alfie. Do we have to?"

I can actually hear him nodding on the other side of the phone. "Yes. Yes, we do."

I get to the tree a few minutes early and thankfully Alfie is already there waiting for me. He walks over to me, smiling his shy smile.

"You OK?"

"My legs are shaking like crazy." I glance around. "Is there any sign yet?"

"Not unless your sister is that pensioner feeding the seagulls." Alfie shrugs. "It's still early."

"I know." I hug my arms to my chest. "I wish I didn't feel so sick."

"This is exciting," he says softly. "Don't be scared."

"I'll try not to be," I whisper. "I just—"

"Alice?"

I look up. The girl standing in front of me is beautiful. Her dark hair is slightly lighter than mine, wavy and hanging loose to her shoulders in a far more tidy style. Her skin is clear and smooth, her eyes are dark and warm. She smiles.

My sister? Really?

"Jas?" I whisper.

She giggles. "Wow – you look like him. Like our dad." She touches my shoulder gently. "I can't believe you're actually here. I'm finally meeting you."

I blink. I don't know what to say. I'm shivering, but in a good way.

"You are so pretty," she says, and I almost laugh.

"No way – look at you! You're so tiny and cute!"

I notice Alfie has slipped back a little. I glance over at him, but he nods softly. "I'll wait here," he says.

Jas gently slips her arm through mine. "Let's sit over there. By the sea," she says. "We have so much to talk about. So much. I don't even know where to begin."

As she leads me to the bench, our footsteps fall in time. It feels so natural. This is my sister.

She is part of me.

We talk for so long. About everything and anything. Time races by and it's not long enough to absorb all the information I want from her. She tells me about her part-time job as a carer. She's doing her A levels and saving up for a car so that she can take her mum out for trips. She talks about her mum, Carmel, quite a bit, who struggles with a back condition, but is kind and funny. Jas tells me that she's single, because "boys do her head in". She talks about her little brother, Ashton, and the amount of grief he gives her.

I ask her about our dad, of course.

"I don't see him," she tells me, quite matter-of-fact. "Not any more. I think I was about five when he finally moved away, not long after you guys left for good." She sighs. "I don't really know what I can tell you about him. He wasn't around much even when he was there. He'd flit in and out of our lives like some kind of homeless cat." She shrugs. "Mum said she loved him once, but not any more. I remember silly little things about him, like he loved singing and he was really good at drawing."

I look up at that. "Really? Did he draw a lot?"

"I remember him doodling and he'd draw me silly pictures sometimes. Mum said that he was really good, so. . ." She sighs again. "It's a shame. I guess we'll never really know, will we? He's just one of those people who should never have been a parent – he wasn't up to the job."

"I guess. . ." I mutter. "It's funny, my mum said the same."

"Well, we were both lucky to have mums that did the job twice as well."

I smile. She's right. I have my mum. My beautiful, kind mum. She is worth twice of any loser dad.

"I have a few photos at home. I can show you if you like," she says gently. "You really do look like him. You have his darker hair. It's a wild look."

"Maybe I am a bit like him..." I say, not knowing if this is a good thing.

"Maybe you just took the good parts of him," she says, grinning.

My cheeks redden. I like the thought of that. I like to think that this man, however useless he might have been, might have gifted me some positive things.

My wild hair, my love of art, my need to be free...

Jas touches my hand. "It's getting late, you know. I need to get back."

"I wish you could stay," I say impulsively.

"This is just the start. We've got plenty of time to find out everything about each other." She grins at me, her eyes glinting. "And I mean *everything*. Why you moved back here, for a start."

I shiver. Just the thought of Ross puts a dampener on everything. Jas seems to notice my change in expression and she nods.

"Well, like I said. We have plenty of time. This is just the beginning. But for now it's getting late. Your poor friend is still waiting for you."

I look over at Alfie. I had actually forgotten

about him and a stab of guilt spikes me, but Alfie is sitting under the tree on his phone. He looks pretty relaxed.

"I'll call you. We can even arrange for our families to meet, if your mum would be happy with that. My mum has wanted to meet you for years. And my brother is a total pain – but I'm sure you'll like him just fine."

"I'm sure I will. I've got a brother too. And a baby sister."

Jas touches my hair gently. "A sister. Just as I imagined, but even better. Perfect."

I am blushing again. I dip my gaze. "I'm not perfect."

"Yes you are. You are my sister and I've found you at last. That makes you perfect," she says firmly.

My sister.

I'm not sure if this is the best day of my life so far, but if it's not it has to come pretty close.

Chapter Eighteen

As we walk back up the hill, I can hardly keep my words inside. They spill from me like an overflowing fountain.

"...did you see how pretty she was? And she's really interesting too. She seemed so relaxed and funny. She was telling me how she looks after old people and she loves it. But that's not what she wants to do for ever. She wants to be a beauty therapist eventually..."

Alfie smiles at me as I gabble on. "She sounds cool."

"Isn't she?" I stop walking for a second. It's

like everything is totally overwhelming me. "I can't believe this, you know? A few days ago I was terrified. I thought everything was going wrong, I thought that Ross was after us . . . but instead. . ."

"You have a new sister," Alfie finishes for me helpfully.

"I have a sister," I repeat.

"It's good to see you so happy. You deserve this, really you do," Alfie says. "I hated seeing you so upset about everything. But now you have something positive to focus on."

He's right. I can start moving forward again, just like Mum wants me to. I can even stop worrying about things like school, because finally I feel like I am beginning to fit somewhere. I do belong.

Everything is slowly falling into place – Jas, Alfie, Ms Monroe, even Lauren. They all offer me a future that I never thought I could have before.

"It's all going to be all right, isn't it, Alfie?" I say. It's not a question, because I finally believe it.

He grins at me anyway. "Of course it is, Alice. Things are really exciting for you right now and do you know what? You deserve it."

He takes my hand and squeezes it, bringing me to a stop. "Who was there for me when I was utterly miserable? Who is one of the best friends I've ever had...? Even though I've only known you, what? Less than a year? Who do I care about so much?"

"Me?" I whisper, fighting back the smile.

"You."

We stand there for a moment, smiling at each other, not saying anything else. He's right. He's my best friend and I'm his. I think I realize for the first time how much that means. How important a true friend is.

"But you know..." Alfie says. "As wonderful as I think you are, there's someone else who is even more besotted."

I blink, frowning up at him.

"Ben," he says softly.

My frown deepens. I pull my hand away.

"You know what I think about him. He totally freaked me out."

Alfie takes back my hand. "I know he went about things the wrong way – but that's Ben. He's awkward and loud and a bit weird sometimes." He pauses. "The strange thing is, he's shy too, even though you wouldn't expect it."

I stare at him and then we both giggle.

"You're really selling him," I say.

"But he's also one of the kindest guys I've ever known." Alfie pauses. "He really, *really* likes you and now he's beating himself up, knowing he upset you. Seriously – you should see the texts he's been sending me!"

"OK..." I say quietly. "I get that he was embarrassed about knocking and I guess he was hoping to run into me in the street. But he should've talked to me. He should've told me what he had done. He could see how worried I was."

Alfie nods. "He knows that. He says he was scared you would hate him for it. He really, really likes you, Alice."

"I like him too," I say. My mind goes back to the drawing I did of him in the art room, of the funny feeling I get in my tummy when I see him. "I think I have for a while."

"Then – will you talk to him again?"

"I guess."

Alfie makes a whooping sound under his breath. "I didn't think I'd get you to agree to that."

"Well. I guess you caught me in a good mood." I look up at him and notice how much his eyes are sparkling. "This really means a lot to you?"

"Are you serious? My two best mates getting along again." Alfie laughs softly. "Nothing would make me happier."

Mum is waiting in the living room and when I push the door fully open I see that she is not alone. Another woman is sitting opposite her. She is curvy, gorgeous, has the brightest red hair I've ever seen and a smile that seems to take over her entire face. She jumps up when I walk into the room.

"Oh my god. Alice!" she says loudly. "I haven't seen you since you were a tiny baby."

I turn to Mum, confused, and see that she is smiling too.

"Alice," she says warmly. "This is my old friend Rainey. I was telling you about her."

Rainey walks over to me and gently touches my face. "I haven't seen you since you were so small. Three or four? I bet you don't even remember me." Her eyes are green and heavily lined with eyeliner. They glint excitedly at me. "You've changed so much – except for your hair, of course. You still have that wonderful, wild hair."

"I think I do remember you. . ." I whisper.

It's her voice more than anything. Loud but still soothing. Immediately I'm swept back in time. An arm is wrapped around me, the same sweet perfume is drifting over me.

"I'll huff and I'll puff. . ."

"Wait – it was you that read 'The Three Little Pigs' to me!" I say.

Not Mum at all. Rainey!

Rainey stares down at me. "You remember? I read that to you every night when your mum needed rest. It was your favourite."

"I used to think it was Mum reading it. But it was you. Of course it was you."

"I missed you so much when your mum

moved away," Rainey says. "But now you're back. Back here where you belong."

The word "belong" floats between us. I want to grab it and hold it in my hand. I want to lock it away in my heart and never let it go again.

"Everything is as it should be now," Mum says, getting up and walking over to us. She is holding Amy on her hip and she gurgles in excitement. "I have my friend back. I have my family with me – safe."

"Where's Henry?" I ask.

"Outside. Building another camp." Mum laughs. "He wants to show Rainey this new one. Let's just say, they get along fine!"

Rainey touches my cheek again. I like the feel of her smooth nails on my skin. It's so familiar.

"Your mum has been telling me all about you," she says. "You've grown into quite an amazing young woman."

I dip my head a little, unsure of what to say.

"She is amazing," Mum says. "And forgiving. What she's been through … what I put her through…"

"It's not your fault, Mum," I say firmly.

"I didn't do enough to keep you safe," Mum says. "But from now on, everything will be different."

"I met Jas," I whisper. "I met her like you told me to."

"Good," Mum says. "You need to do that. It's the right thing to do."

"You really don't mind?"

"I don't mind, Alice. I'll never mind. I want you to be happy, that's all. After everything – we need to be with people who love us." She swallows. "Alice, I have so much to tell you. I feel like my past has been a closed door to you. I've always found it so hard to open up, but I want to change. I want you to know all about me. But it'll will take some time, is that OK?"

I nod, fighting back the tears again. "Of course it is, Mum."

"This house. Your friends. . ." Rainey adds. "It really is a new chapter for you both."

Mum snorts a little. "Well – I'm not sure about the house part. You used to go on about the smell."

I quickly lift my hand up to silence her. "I don't even notice it any more, Mum. It's gone."

And it's true. I can't remember the last time I worried about it.

The house smells of food cooking and the baby and Rainey's sweet perfume.

This house is perfect.

I think it always was.

It's later that evening when there's knock on the door.

I open the door, and there's Ben.

"Hey," he says shyly.

He looks awkward standing there, with his crazy hair and shaven eyebrow. But still kind of cute.

I take him out to the back garden where it's quiet. As we pass the stairs I can hear Mum and Rainey reading Henry a bedtime story together. It's not "The Three Little Pigs".

We sit together on the low wall and it's a while before either of us speak. I want him to say something first. I think he owes me that.

"I'm sorry," he says finally. "That's what I came here to say. I'm sorry. I messed up badly."

"That's OK," I tell him. "Thank you though, for apologizing."

He nods slowly.

"Are you OK?" he asks. "Alfie told me you met your sister and it went really well. And that you talked to your mum. . ."

"Yeah," I say. "Everything is going to be OK, I think." I take a deep breath. "I still don't understand why you were so scared to come to my door. I mean, we're friends, aren't we?"

"Yeah. Yeah, of course we are."

"Then what was so scary?"

"Well. . ." He stares at his feet. "I know we're mates but I wasn't thinking of you that way any more. I mean, I was thinking of you as something else. More than a mate."

I laugh. "Ben. You're really not good at this, are you?"

Ben looks up at me. His cheeks are bright red. "Can you tell?" he says, and smiles shyly.

"Did you want to ask me out?" I say.

His smile grows a little. "Yeah. Yeah, I did. I had all these amazing things practised that I was going to say to you and everything."

I can feel myself flushing too. "Like what?"

"Like... Like how you're fearless and beautiful. And strong. And a bit wild. And funny and beautiful ... did I just say that?"

"Yeah ... I think so," I reply, feeling a bit embarrassed. "That's lovely, Ben. But I'm none of those things."

"Oh, you are," he says, suddenly sounding confident. "But the best thing is – you don't even realize it."

He reaches over and takes my hand. It's so warm and soft in mine. I shuffle a bit closer. He releases his hand and pulls me into a hug instead. I shiver. This is nice. Really nice.

"Maybe you could've just have texted me," I say. "You know? Like anyone else would?"

"But that's just the thing. I didn't want to be like everyone else. I wanted to do something special." He grins. "I put it all in the letter. It was a really good one, honest. I explained everything. I only wish you'd seen it."

"Aw." I bite my lip, looking at his hopeful face and his lopsided eyebrow. How Ben thinks he could be like anyone else is quite something. I wish I'd seen the letter too. "OK. I get it. Maybe you could write another one – one day."

"So . . . maybe we could go out?" He squeezes my hand. "I really am sorry. I would never have wanted to scare you like that. I promise I never will again."

I squeeze his hand back. "I know," I whisper. "And yeah, I think we could go out."

He kisses the top of my head and it's so sweet, so perfect that I want to cry. But of course I don't. Instead I allow myself to enjoy the moment. It's nice.

For once, it all feels good.

"Everything is coming together," I whisper instead.

"Do you think?" he says.

"Yeah. Yeah, I do."

He pulls me in tighter against him. "I think you're right."

A light breeze curls through the trees. I watch as it gently lifts up the sheet that Henry has used for his new makeshift tent. This is his new improved version, a tent that can deter monsters. He said this one was unbreakable. He said no baddies could get him in this one. He said this time we are totally safe.

Who knows. Maybe he's right.

"If you could be any animal, what would you be?" I ask suddenly.

Ben thinks for a moment. "I'd be a wolf, I think. A wolf with a really funky hairstyle so that I stand out from the rest of the pack. What about you?"

"A bird," I say, straight away. "I'll be a bird, an interesting one with colours on its wing. Maybe a magpie. I'd fly wherever I wanted to and I'd never be afraid."

"That sounds good," Ben replies.

"But I'll still have a nest," I add. "A place I can come back to whenever I need to."

Because I can fly all I want. I can be free.

But I'll always need a place to call home.

Also by Eve Ainsworth:

Turn over for an extract...

Chapter One

Seven o'clock in the morning and the house was an empty shell. The door to Dad's room stood open, like a hungry gaping mouth. The bed was neatly made, and everything was tidied away just as it should be. I stood for a moment at the door, looking in, feeling that heavy dread coiled inside my stomach. It was stupid. I knew he had to leave early today but it didn't stop the uneasy feeling, the same old worry drip-feeding into my gut. The house was full of echoes and space and I didn't like it.

In fact, I hated it.

There is something about this house when it's empty. It is hard to describe but it always unsettles me – like bony fingers scratching at the back of my neck, daring me to turn around and look deep into the shadows to see the things I am afraid to see. The things that are no longer there.

The missing stuff.

The gaps.

It makes me want to be a little kid again, run under the bed and hide. Or to get far away and not be here at all. It was too still. I wanted noise, a little bit of madness.

I just wanted something else.

I got dressed and went downstairs. The doors sat closed. Shadows drifted in the corners and around the edges. I swear it never used to be this cold and dark. He'd left out my breakfast as usual. A packet of cereal and a bowl. No note, of course. I could see his unfinished mug of coffee on the drainer. Other than that, the kitchen was completely tidy – untouched, almost. Unlived-in. I glanced at the cereal for a second, wondering if I could be bothered to eat, but my stomach felt too tight and small. I scanned the room, considering the options – the small loaf of bread poking out of the bread bin, the few remaining biscuits in the jar. It was no use. I needed to get out of there.

I picked up my bag, plucked the keys from the bowl in the hall and slammed out of the front door. I tried to ignore the overgrown grass and Dad's neglected bike leaning against the fence. It never used to be like this, and if I got away from here and concentrated really hard, I could pretend it still wasn't.

Despite my thoughts, my body was under protest as I dragged it down the path that winds along the side of our house. I guess most of me still wanted to be in bed. In truth, I was probably mad to be out of the house so early. But what choice did I have? Stay inside, in there, alone, or be outside, away from it all. I felt like a ghost walking in the weak morning light. It was still so dark. My school bag pulled hard on my muscles where I'd slung it over my shoulder. There was no one else around – no dog walkers, not even that mad jogger who lives at the other end of the road. I breathed in hard, taking in large lungfuls of air, trying to wake myself. The autumn air was sharp and crisp. The leaves crunched under my feet, breaking into dust.

Dust to dust. . .

The path turned a sharp left behind the house and followed a muddy track between bushes and tall, spindly trees. I could walk this in the pitch black and not fall, it is so familiar to me. Every stone, every dip, every tree root. I pushed up, shoving aside the overgrown branches. The route runs alongside the allotments and was dead at that time of morning – although I was pretty sure I could see some movement on the patch in the far corner. Maybe I wasn't the only weirdo up and about.

On the opposite side of the path is the small park for kids. My eyes scanned the fenced area quickly: the small blue slide, the baby swings, the climbing frame that had once seemed impossibly tall. I turned my head away. I'd not been in that place for years. It was part of the past. I reached the small, rotting stile at the end of the path, stumbling over it with my bag banging heavily against my side. The ground was pretty boggy on the other side and I cursed under my breath as my foot planted nicely into a huge muddy puddle. But I carried on nonetheless, ploughing ahead uphill, across the field, walking faster. I preferred this route. OK, it was a little longer, but it was more interesting. And quieter. I might bump into the occasional dog-walker, but that would be about it. And thankfully none of them would be interested in speaking to me.

At the top, the slope flattened into the playing field, and I stopped to take a few deep breaths. The old goalposts stood at the far side. This was the place where we always went to play. Actually, the others still go there. Why wouldn't they? Nothing has changed for them. I remembered what it felt like to just turn up here, dump my stuff and throw myself into a game.

Something tugged at my stomach, and I blinked hard. I quickly turned the other way. I could see it now.

The sea.

I kept walking till I was clear of the grass and on the promenade. The road was practically empty as I crossed it and made my way over to the railings and along to the furthest blue bench, the one nearest the broken-down pier that stretches out to sea. This was my place. *Our* place. Where we'd always gone.

Me and Mum.

She said it was a tiny piece of paradise. Maybe that was going too far, but it *was* special. To us, anyway. The grey, rolling waves crashed in welcome; the salt air whipped around me, freezing my face and numbing my lips. It was an odd mixture of quiet and noisy there. You could be totally alone, and yet you weren't. The sea has a way of making you feel part of it.

I felt myself relax.

Carefully I leant up against the railings. The iron was cool and hard against my back. Now I could really concentrate. I could really listen. And they were calling, of course – the birds. And today I was determined to be there. To be with them again.

I lifted my head and waited.

They came – slowly at first, but soon within my sight: swooping, shrieking seagulls. They didn't seem to mind me. One even landed a few metres away, his wings stretched out wide in a crooked kind of greeting. His head tilted slightly and his beady eyes regarded me with curiosity.

"Morning," I whispered, my words seeming to fizz on the cold air. "It's good to see you, mate."

I swear he tipped his head a little more, his beak turning towards me. Was I going mad?

"She always said—"

"Who are you talking to?"

I froze. For the briefest of moments, that voice threw me. It was too familiar. I shifted position, turned around. But of course it wasn't her. It was someone else – just some girl, standing there staring, her hand resting against the lamp post behind me. I definitely didn't recognize her. She looked young, much younger than me. And she was so thin she could've blended into the railings I was standing by. Her dark hair was wild and the wind whipped it around her pale, white face, and around her darkly made-up eyes. She had a bright, red smile. Her eyes sparkled as she caught my gaze.

"Were you talking to yourself?" she asked again bluntly. Her voice was loud against the breeze.

I blinked. The seagull had gone now, stupid traitor, so it obviously looked like I had been talking to myself. Mind you, was it any better to admit that I had been whispering to a manky old bird?

"What's it got to do with you?" I said, getting up quickly. I didn't need this. I didn't want anyone else around. Why was she even here at this hour? It was so early. Too early for people like her. I came here at this time for that very reason, because I didn't want to see anyone. I didn't want to be bothered.

"Bit weird, that's all. . ." she muttered.

I glared back at her. Was she for real? Staring at me like that, while she was dressed in some shabby grey T-shirt and shapeless jeans. She looked like she'd dug her clothes out of a bin. And wasn't she cold? She didn't even have a coat on. I flinched. Was she OK?

But I didn't have time for this. Not now. I needed to be on my own. I shook my head slowly, hitching my bag over my shoulder.

"So why are you here?" she said.

"I just am . . . no reason. . ."

"Nice." She grinned. "You're dead friendly, you are."

I shrugged. "Sorry. . ."

I started to move away. "I'm not weird," I said as I passed her. After all, I wasn't the one standing in the cold spying on other people. I wasn't the one who needed to brush my hair. And I wasn't the one dressed for summer on an icy morning.

"Hey!" she shouted, but I didn't want to talk to her. I didn't want *anyone*. I only wanted the seagull and she had scared it away.

So, thanks for that.

He was too excited, dressed in his new football kit. He kicked a cushion across the floor, watching it skid and turn. He loved his new boots the best. They were yellow and green and had been his favourite ones in the shop. He had got them as a reward for his hat trick last week. His mum always knew which ones he liked the most. She liked treating him.

"Hey watch it, Ronaldo!" she laughed. "I don't want you smashing up the house."

She was gathering up his bag, his drink, his shin pads. Outside it was pouring hard with rain, but neither of them cared.

"Let's go!" she yelled.

They ran to the car, giggling and shrieking as the rain splattered against their faces. She moaned about the weather making her hair even more "wild", but her complaints didn't seem that real. She was smiling all the time. On the short drive he couldn't stop talking. What would this team be like? Was he good enough to play for them? What if he played badly? His mum simply smiled at him through the rear-view mirror.

"You'll be fine," she said. "You're my little star."

They parked up and strode across the muddy

field towards a large man with a red, ruddy face. He stepped forwards and held out his hand for shaking.

"Alfie. I've heard good things about you. Your mum says you have quite a talent."

He looked up. His mum was beaming. She ruffled his hair.

"He's only eight but he's been playing above his age for two years now at Rushfield. But it's time for new challenges. I've heard this is the best team."

The man grinned. "Indeed. And we need a good midfielder."

"Is Dad not coming?" Alfie asked her.

She shook her head. "He has to work. But he's dead proud too." She leant in close "But not as proud as me," she whispered in his ear.

"Come on," said his new coach. "I'll introduce you to the rest of the team."

He paused, feeling that little twist of anxiety that often pulled him back.

Could he really do this?

He looked back at his mum and she just nodded gently.

"It'll be fine, Alfie. I'm here. I'm not leaving you."

She was right. Of course she was right. He knew that she would be watching him the whole time. She wasn't going anywhere.